"Then how about a walk?" her handsome host offered. "Maybe that'll work up your appetite for coffee and dessert."

She managed a negligible nod as he moved around the table and pulled back her chair.

But it wasn't until he took her hand and led her outside into the moonlight that she knew she was in serious trouble.

"I'll bet you don't have stars like this in Chicago," he suggested as he peered up at the sky.

Amy started to answer, but the view took away her ability to speak as well as her breath. The black canvas of the night sky spread out endlessly before her. Stars glistened like diamonds splashed across its vast velvet surface.

Oh, yes, he would be right about that. Apparently there were a good many things down here in Texas that she didn't have back home—would never have. Those sexy blue eyes locked with her hungry ones and awareness quivered across her heated skin like the greedy fingers of a skilled lover.

And that was precisely why she had to say goodnight with no possibility of coffee or dessert.

She was far too sure that the dessert would be way more than she was prepared to accept.

Way, way more.

Dear Reader,

Welcome to the COLBY AGENCY! In this story you'll meet a cowboy and oil tycoon named John Calhoun from the great state of Texas. If you've read my COLBY AGENCY stories before you'll recognize Amy Wells, the agency's spunky receptionist. Amy's top priority is to become a private investigator, but she's certain no one will take her seriously until she proves herself. Come along on this journey with Amy and John and find out just how much trouble one little lady can get herself into when she sets her mind to it.

I hope you'll look for more of my COLBY AGENCY stories wherever Harlequin Intrigue books are sold.

Happy reading and, as always, let me hear from you at P.O. Box 64, Huntland, Tennessee 37345. Also, visit my Web site at www.debrawebb.com.

God bless!

Debra Webb

ROMANCING THE TYCOON
Debra Webb

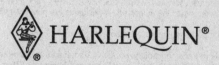

HARLEQUIN®

TORONTO • NEW YORK • LONDON
AMSTERDAM • PARIS • SYDNEY • HAMBURG
STOCKHOLM • ATHENS • TOKYO • MILAN • MADRID
PRAGUE • WARSAW • BUDAPEST • AUCKLAND

ISBN 0-373-75015-3

ROMANCING THE TYCOON

Chapter One

Amy Wells flipped to the next page of her *Glamour* magazine: ''The Perfect Man…''

She lifted a skeptical eyebrow at the perfect-man assets listed by women between the ages of eighteen and thirty polled by the sassy magazine. Tall, broad-shouldered, well-muscled and sinfully handsome. That about summed it up, she mused. What guy who looked like that wouldn't fit the profile?

One word…that's all it took to send her mood back into a depressive state.

Profile. She wanted to do profiles…to work undercover. To be a Colby Agency investigator.

She sighed woefully. She'd given up on the fairy tale. She wasn't going to find Mr. Right or Mr. Perfect. Though she was only twenty-five, she longed for a steady, satisfying relationship. It just wasn't happening. And it wasn't just her. Lots of her friends had the same problem. Where were all the good men?

They no longer existed, she had decided, and promptly she'd thrown herself into her job. If she couldn't have a great sex life with the man of her dreams, she could at least have a great job. So far she'd managed to come a long way. She'd been hired by the Colby Agency, the most prestigious private investigations firm in the state, if not the country. She'd worked her way from receptionist to personal assistant. But she longed for more. She wanted to be a real agent, to track down the answers…the bad guys.

Another wistful sigh seeped past her lips as she stuffed the magazine back into her desk drawer. Break time was over. No more fantasizing for today. Time to get back to the real world.

Amy glanced forlornly at the stack of folders to be sorted and filed. Though she appreciated very much her latest promotion to personal assistant, it wasn't enough. Mildred, Victoria Colby-Camp's loyal secretary, was a great lady to work for, but Amy longed for so much more.

She'd read every single final report on every case the Colby Agency had taken on in the past three years. At first, she'd been content to serve as receptionist and merely watch with growing interest as the investigators the agency employed went about their intriguing business. To be honest, she'd been a little intimidated by the likes of Ian Michaels and Simon Ruhl. But then a new female investigator had been hired, Nicole Reed-Michaels. That had changed everything for Amy.

Though Amy had heard about the agency's first female investigator, Katherine Robertson, who'd married the infamous secret agent Jack Raine, watching one in action was a whole other ball game. Nicole's supreme intelligence and slick, super-agent demeanor had kindled an unquenchable passion in Amy to follow in her esteemed footsteps.

Amy wanted to be a Colby agent. She wanted a case of her own. One where she would uncover the identity of the bad guy. Where she would save the day and make Victoria proud.

She wanted to be one of the best.

If only she could somehow garner the boss's attention in that light. She'd started taking self-defense classes about a year ago and was pretty good if she did say so herself. She'd also sharpened her observation skills by teaching herself to pay attention to even the smallest detail. She'd even signed up for a private investigator class at the local spy shop. She'd learned all kinds of interesting things there and just by listening around the office. It wasn't as though she had dates lining up to fill her calendar.

What more could she do?

She was twenty-five! Time was running out. Before long her best years would be behind her and she wouldn't have accomplished the one thing she wanted more than anything else: to be a Colby agent.

The magazine in her drawer nagged at her. Okay, so she still wanted to meet the right guy as well. But she realized now that her first priority was getting her career on track. She'd thought long and hard about it and had realized what could happen if she fell in love first. Certainly there was nothing wrong with falling in love. Even the venerable Colby agents fell in love on a regular basis, most of the time while on a case.

A dreamy smile slid across Amy's face. Now that would just about make things perfect. Getting her career headed in the right direction while at the same time finding the perfect man. Instantly her heart rate picked up an extra beat.

But then, that probably wouldn't happen. It just made her feel better to believe that her career kept her too busy to think about her social life. And hoping against hope that her career would kick in at the same time that she'd meet the man of her dreams was a nice fantasy.

Oh well, it kept the cynicism at bay.

The telephone on her desk buzzed, summoning her back to earth for a cold, hard reality check.

She was still a personal assistant. And finding the perfect man was about as likely as was stumbling onto the precise case that would finally get Victoria's attention.

Waiting for hell to freeze over was a wiser bet.

"Amy Wells," she said automatically, answering the telephone before it buzzed for the second time.

"The Hanover file?" Amy listened as Mildred confirmed the name of the file she needed. "Right away," she said in answer to the request that it be brought to her office as soon as possible.

Pushing her troubling thoughts aside, Amy went off to the records room in search of the Hanover file. Her fantasy might never become a reality, but at least she could keep dreaming. There was no law against that or any statute of limitations. To hell with admitting defeat, she'd just keep reaching for the brass ring.

With that in mind, her imagination instantly conjured a shadowy image of the perfect man. One who was everything the magazine poll said he should be and more. A grin tugged at her lips as she opened the drawer labeled *H* and flipped through the folders. One who needed rescuing by a woman like her.

Amy Wells, Colby agent-in-training.

"GOOD MORNING, Edgar," Victoria Colby-Camp said when her call was transferred to her impatient client. Edgar Winterborne had requested a rush on the background check of his prospective son-in-law, Texas oil tycoon John Robert Calhoun, IV.

"I hope you have good news for me, Victoria," he said urgently. "There's a lot riding on this deal."

His one and only daughter's future, Victoria silently filled in for him. Edgar Winterborne was about to pull off the merger of the century. Winterborne Industries of Illinois and Calhoun Oil of Texas were on the verge of becoming the Cal-Borne Alliance. The two families had been sworn enemies since before the Civil War. But the differences in the two went far deeper than North versus South, they were about money. The almighty dollar. Whoever had the most was in control.

And Edgar Winterborne's somewhat spoiled daughter, as well as the Calhoun heir, were caught slap in the middle of it all.

"You can rest easy, Edgar," Victoria told him. "John Calhoun is as clean as they come. His business dealings as well as his personal ones are as honest as they are impressive. If the man has a single skeleton in his closet, it's not to be found.'' That was one thing Victoria would stake her agency's reputation on, thoroughness. The investigation into the Calhoun family had revealed many things: wealth, power and a strong hand in politics, but not one aspect leaned even remotely toward the negative. The Calhouns were a fine family, as were the Winterbornes. Victoria simply didn't understand the motivation for the current no-holds-barred merger. Why couldn't they just get along and do what had to be done within the business of refining oil without involving blood?

"This is very important to me,'' Edgar interjected solemnly. "As much as I want this deal to happen, I want my daughter to be safe and happy.''

"I'm certain you do,'' Victoria allowed for lack of anything else to say. Arranged marriages just weren't heard of anymore. Certainly not in the United States of America. That either of the participants would be willing still amazed her. Then again, money could be a powerful motivator. She sincerely hoped it would prove to be about more than the money. Marriages fell apart everyday with partners who considered themselves to be in love. What hope could there be for a couple who hadn't even met? She prayed they would work those details out before children were brought into the picture.

A child didn't need that kind of uncertainty. Victoria knew that all too well. Children needed love, nurturing and support. Anything less left a permanent mark. She had been robbed of the opportunity to protect and nurture her own son. But he was back now and she intended to make up for every moment they had missed.

"I'll be happy to have a copy of the report delivered to your home this afternoon," she said, interrupting Edgar's rambling about the price of crude and how it would take a strong American alliance to end this country's dependence on foreign oil.

"That would be splendid. We're planning on spending a few days down in Texas starting this evening," he told her. "I'd like to take a look at that report before we leave."

"I'll have it delivered straight away then," Victoria offered. "I'm sure Regina is looking forward to the trip." Regina was Edgar's daughter, the one whose life was about to change vastly. From all reports the young woman was quite a handful. She'd dropped out of three different colleges before completing her education. Her father had bailed her out of numerous financial scrapes and unsavory liaisons with exboyfriends. Victoria wasn't certain for whom she felt the most sympathy, Regina Winterborne or John Calhoun, her prospective groom.

"I appreciate that, Victoria," Edgar said. "I can always count on the Colby Agency."

And that was the bottom line as far as Victoria was concerned. The Colby Agency always came through. "Thank you, Edgar. Have a pleasant trip to Texas." With that the call ended and Victoria pressed the buzzer for Mildred. "Ask Amy to step into my office, please."

"Will do," Mildred returned pleasantly.

Victoria's brow furrowed with worry as she waited

for Amy's arrival. Mildred had been her secretary since the Colby Agency's inception. She did not want to lose her, but Victoria had a feeling that as Mildred's relationship progressed with her current beau, Dr. Austin Ballard, that possibility became more and more likely. Dr. Ballard had already retired and turned his pharmaceuticals company over to his daughter Jennifer. His one desire now was to enjoy each day and to travel—with the new love in his life, Victoria feared selfishly. She considered asking Ethan Delaney, one of her top investigators, to talk to Jennifer. After all, she was his wife. He'd rescued both Jennifer and her father from the evil that had threatened them not so long ago. It was at Ethan and Jennifer's wedding that Mildred had met Dr. Ballard. Maybe, Victoria reflected, she'd have a little chat with Ethan later today.

Just then Amy Wells entered the room, her smile bright, her expression eager. As always her appearance was professional yet very hip. She wore a pair of hip-hugger khakis and a slim-fitting navy sweater that just met the wide leather belt accentuating the low-riding slacks as well as her slender hips. Her long dark hair looked silky, the straight style quite youthful. But it was her brown eyes that shone above all else. Amy was bright and always, always polite.

Though Victoria considered Amy an asset to the agency, somehow she just couldn't see her as Mildred's replacement should that necessity arise. It wasn't for lack of ability, Victoria knew. Amy's heart just didn't appear to be in the world of clerical duties. Though she always did an outstanding job, whether she was filing or interacting with the clientele, still, something was missing.

Inspiration, Victoria decided. Amy was not inspired by her work and that troubled Victoria. They would have to talk. Soon.

"How are you today, Amy?" she said, forcing away the lines of concern with a heartfelt smile.

"Fine, Victoria. How can I help you?"

Victoria studied her for one moment more before she relayed her needs. There was a hopefulness about her that gave Victoria pause. Maybe they should have that talk now. But, she remembered, Edgar Winterborne needed the report right away—in time to review it before leaving for Texas.

Her usual keen focus fractured, Victoria shuffled the pages of the report together and slid them into a large white envelope. After penning Edgar's name and address on the front, she pressed the clasp into place and offered the closed envelope to Amy.

"Mr. Winterborne is waiting for this report. I'd like you to hand-carry it to his residence. Deliver it personally to him."

Amy nodded. "Sure. Anything else?"

Again that hopeful flicker of something just beneath the surface. Concern drew a new line between Victoria's eyebrows. "Is there something we need to discuss, Amy?" Despite the shortness of time, she simply couldn't send her away without asking.

A mask of uncertainty instantly claimed the young woman's features. "Everything's fine, ma'am," she said hesitantly. "Was there anything else you needed?"

Confident there was more, but, considering the shortness of time, willing to let it go, Victoria nodded. "That's all." She watched Amy hurry away. It was past time she got to the bottom of this. With the possibility of Mildred taking an extended leave or worse, Victoria couldn't afford to have Amy unhappy. She was the only person at the agency who knew the many secrets of how Mildred accomplished her numerous and varied tasks. No way could Victoria risk losing them both, and she certainly couldn't stand in the way of true love.

The blessing—or curse depending upon the way one looked at it—of true love without fail found her investigators one by one. No matter how they tried to evade it, it always homed in on its target. Case in point, Trevor Sloan. Now there had been a man who definitely was not looking for love—true or otherwise. But it had located him just the same.

Victoria exhaled a long sigh of defeat. Why fight it? It was inevitable. Sometimes she lost a valued employee, sometimes she gained one. It all evened out in the end, she supposed.

Besides, who was she to fight true love? It certainly had found her—twice in her life. Lucas Camp, her beloved husband, immediately came to mind, sending a stir of heat through her. Though James Colby, her first husband and father of her son, would always hold a special place in her heart, Lucas made her incredibly happy. If only all couples contemplating a future together could find what she and Lucas had discovered…true love firmly based on absolute trust.

The Wild Horse Ranch…near Runaway Bay, Texas

JOHN ROBERT CALHOUN, IV, sat astride his mount in the middle of a wide-open pasture and watched the beautiful horses graze. Shiny brown and black coats, a few dappled and mottled whites, all with perfect proportion and carriage. The Wild Horse Ranch was lucky to have such an awesome herd. He blinked and looked out over the endless sea of green pasture. But it wasn't horses that made the Calhoun name the respected one it was. Nope. It was the thousands of acres of oil fields that lay beyond what the eye could see. It was the crude pumped every day from deep within the earth. Black gold. In Texas, oil equated to royalty.

"God Almighty," John muttered. Did it really need to be this way?

"I understand your misgivings, John," the solemn voice said from next to him.

Nathanial Beckman, Nate, had followed him out here. The man, his father's closest confidant, wasn't going to let go until he was sure John intended to do his father's bidding once again. Nate had been with the family for forty years and, to John's knowledge, he had never failed in any endeavor.

John lifted his hat and plowed a hand through his hair. "I don't think you do." He settled the Stetson back on his head and shook it slowly from side to side. "He's asking too much this time."

"John." Nate moved his own mount a little closer, his tone more urgent now. "You have to know what a huge step this is, not just for Calhoun Oil but for the whole country."

There he went again with the guilt trip. If Calhoun Oil and Winterborne Industries merged, the country's dependence on foreign oil could be greatly reduced. Both companies stood to gain tremendously and, for the first time in three or four generations, the families would be united. Just what he needed, the weight of the country's oil future as well as the family's one opportunity to set the past to rights resting squarely on his shoulders. Was it his fault that more than a hundred years ago the two families had been torn apart by war and greed and that the rift hadn't been fused to this day?

No it wasn't.

But his father had slam-dunked him with that very burden.

"I know how big it is," he growled, wishing like hell that Nate would find himself something to do while John thought over this whole mess. It wasn't as if it would go away. He had to deal with it…but he needed time to come to terms with what his father wanted him to do.

Marriage.

He bit back a curse. It wasn't that he wanted never to get married. He did. Eventually. But he'd scarcely turned thirty. Why did it have to be now? And to a woman he had never even met?

To seal the merger of a lifetime.

That's what his father would say. The only way that the Winterbornes and the Calhouns would ever be re-united was with a marriage and the co-mingling of blood. In other words—kids. He not only had to marry this woman, he also had to have children with her—posthaste.

This time John did swear. Nate flinched but didn't run away as John wished he would. Instead, he remained steadfastly by, waiting to plead his case once more if need be.

But John didn't have to hear it again. He knew the deal.

Regina Winterborne, twenty-four, had been in more trouble than he could shake a stick at. She was attractive and she wore her highbrow upbringing like a badge of honor. In other words, she was a snob. One who spent a small fortune on designer clothes and who'd had more short-term relationships than even John had. And that was saying something.

Money aside, John had been blessed with an excellent blend of his mother's beauty and his father's rugged features; he knew he was good-looking. How could he not? Women flocked to him as though he was the latest motion picture heartthrob. Most of the time he didn't mind. But occasionally he did. How the hell was he supposed to know the real thing when it came along? Would he really know when a woman cared about him simply for him rather than for his looks or his money? Probably not.

That was one thing he wouldn't have to worry about anymore if he went through with his father's ''deal.'' He would know that the union was about money and the question would be moot. But what kind of life was that? How would children fare with a mother and father who had only married to combine their companies? Not too well, he imagined.

But it wasn't as if he had a lot of options. Though John had recently turned thirty, he had never once in his life disobeyed his father. Not a single time had he ever even considered going against his father's wishes. And, the truth was, he wasn't stupid. He fully understood how important this merger was, on a professional level as well as on several others.

It was the opportunity his father had hoped for, as had his own father and grandfather before him. Not once had they gotten this close. Now the road to reuniting the two most powerful oil companies in the nation lay directly in front of John. Turning away from it was out of the question.

"When will she be here?"

"I'm leaving in half an hour to personally escort the Winterbornes to Texas. We should arrive by five this evening," Nate said proudly. "A quiet dinner at the house has been arranged. Some free time will be available for you and Miss Winterborne since your fathers will be attending the poker game in Runaway Bay later tonight."

The poker game. Not a Friday night had passed in John's lifetime that his father hadn't attended the poker game in Runaway Bay. No less than half a dozen players, all oil barons, showed up for the game each week. John wondered vaguely how the good old boys from Texas would tolerate a Yankee in their midst. A grin tugged at his lips. Maybe this weekend would be worth the trouble after all.

And that easily the decision was made. John would not stand in the way of progress. Nor would he be responsible for another hundred years of antagonism between his family and the Winterbornes. Nope. If a wedding was what it took to pull off this coup, then he'd suit up for the challenge. He wasn't a quitter, and he damn sure never shirked his duty. As the one and only heir of the Calhoun name, he was it. There was no one else to do what had to be done, and another heir was necessary to carry on the family business.

But about one thing he would have his way. The woman who was to be his wife would be *his* wife. His alone. There would be no illicit lovers on the side, no trysts…no cheating whatsoever. It would be the real thing. In and out of bed.

He blew out a mighty breath. "All right, Nate. Let's make this thing happen."

John turned away from the beauty of the horses and the lush pasture and set his sights on something far less attractive—coming to terms with his impending marriage.

Back in Chicago…

AMY MANEUVERED her ancient but reliable car through Chicago's Friday-afternoon traffic more quickly than she'd anticipated and headed to the country estate of Edgar Winterborne. She relaxed her tense shoulders and settled in for the drive once on the open road. All she had to do was deliver this report. She glanced at the white envelope lying on the seat next to her. Then she could call it a day. Mildred had told her not to worry about coming back to the office. Amy could start her Fourth of July weekend early.

She heaved a discontented sigh. Why hadn't she

answered Victoria's question truthfully? How was she ever going to work up the nerve to say what she really wanted? It was so simple. It wasn't as though the possibility of her becoming a full-fledged investigator was beyond the scope of comprehension. She knew she could do it.

All she had to do was prove it somehow.

But there was nothing she could do about it today. It was Friday and Monday was a holiday. She might as well put it out of her mind and enjoy the long weekend. Maybe between now and Tuesday some sort of epiphany would hit and she would know just what to do. Or maybe some handsome stranger would move into the empty apartment across the hall and invite her to help him settle in.

Yeah, right.

The envelope Victoria had given her snagged her attention once more. She looked at her watch. The trip to the Winterbornes would take at least another hour, she might as well make a fuel stop. Then she'd have a chance to take a look at that report. Why not? She read *all* the Colby Agency reports. No one had told her she couldn't.

Banishing the guilt factor to the farthest corner of her mind, she pulled into the lot of the next gas station and parked near the pump. Once the nozzle was in place and the gasoline filling her tank, she climbed back into her car and opened the clasp on the envelope containing the report.

John Robert Calhoun, IV. She surveyed the picture of the Texas cowboy and her mind immediately dredged up the list the glamour magazine poll had compiled. Tall. Mm-hmm. Broad-shouldered. Yep. Well-muscled. She studied the pictures that had been taken without the subject's knowledge. He sat astride a horse and was, apparently, rounding up a herd of horses. Holy-moly—he was gorgeous. A little shiver went through her, awakening a long-slumbering libido. Now there was a real man.

She remembered hearing Victoria tell Mildred that his ranch was called the Wild Horse because he took in the wild animals from all around the country to keep poachers from harming them. A hero. Hmmm. Compassionate and definitely well-muscled, she decided after studying his image awhile longer. And sinfully handsome without a question. His blond hair and blue eyes contrasted sharply with his deeply tanned skin.

He looked like the kind of cowboy who could make any woman swoon. The perfect man. Oh, yeah. Amy sighed wistfully. Lucky Regina Winterborne. He was all hers.

She shook her head and shoved the report back into the envelope. What did she care about hard-bodied cowboys anyway? Focus. She had to stay focused. Right now she had one thing on her mind and one thing only: becoming the next Colby Agency investigator.

Regrettably, she didn't have time for anything else…even fantasizing about a rugged cowboy who was promised to another woman.

Chapter Two

Regina Winterborne was many things. Spoiled, admittedly. Impetuous, definitely. But dumb she was not. She had no intention of marrying some stubborn, macho cowboy. No matter what her daddy promised her.

Living a whole hour outside of Chicago was bad enough. It made hair salon appointments as well as spa sessions immensely annoying. Every time she wanted the least little thing she had to drive all the way into the city. She hated driving into the city. She hated living in the country more.

But she'd tried taking her own apartment in town. The penthouse she'd selected had been opulent without doubt. Her staff of three—cook, maid and personal assistant—had been top notch. The only drawback had been the money. There was never enough of it.

Her father had insisted that if she were going to live away from home she would learn to do so on a budget. So he'd set her up on a monthly allowance. Well, she huffed as she remembered the ridiculously paltry amount, how was she supposed to conduct herself properly under such conditions? Why, there'd scarcely been anything left to pay the hired help each month. So, she'd had to move back home and play the dutiful daughter whenever her father was around.

She folded her arms over her chest and glared out the floor-to-ceiling window of his study. Anything to keep from having to look him directly in the eye. He read her too easily. She wasn't about to let him see what she really thought just now.

"Regina, don't turn your back on me," he ordered in that booming voice that made the board of directors at Winterborne Industries sit up and take notice.

She simply rolled her eyes. "I'm not turning my back on you, Daddy. I'm merely enjoying the fabulous view." And it *was* fabulous, if one was into miles of sickeningly lovely landscape and nothing else.

He moved up beside her, obviously content with her lie. "This is for your own good, my dear. I only want the best for you."

Yeah, right. He wanted to seal this history-making deal and get her out of his hair at the same time. "I'm sure you do." She wasn't entirely successful at keeping a hint of sarcasm out of her tone.

"I know what you're thinking," he said more quietly.

That couldn't possibly be true, she mused, or he'd be ranting rather than gentling his usually boisterous voice. Because right now the only thing she was thinking was how much she wished someone would rescue her from this prison.

Someone like Kevin. Her heart skipped a beat. But Kevin was long gone. He'd quickly grown weary of her father's interference in their relationship…just like all the others.

"You're thinking," her father went on, "that I just want you married off so someone else will have to attend to your needs."

Give the man a cigar. She gritted her teeth, holding back those very words.

"But that's not true at all," he urged. "You're my only daughter—my only child. I want the very best for you." He sighed mightily. "I worry that you'll fall victim to the charms of some no-account like that Kevin Martin. He's worthless."

Regina didn't have to look to know that her father's face had turned beet-red, she could hear his temper rising in his voice. He hated Kevin. Had hated all her boyfriends from the time she was fourteen and had developed breasts as well as a mind of her own.

Well, that was just too bad. He was not going to pick her husband. She would not be forced into an arranged marriage.

"If your mother were here, she'd tell you the same thing," her father said more calmly. "Men like Martin are leeches—self-serving and uncaring about anyone but themselves. He isn't nearly good enough for you. I hope you see that."

"Yes, Daddy," she lied again, just to get him off the subject. "I know that Kevin is scum. You don't have to worry. He broke up with me anyhow."

That much was the truth. Kevin had tired of the run-ins with her father and had opted to run out on her. She stiffened her spine against the unfairness of it all. And now her father wanted her to marry some cowboy just because he had the largest oil business in Texas. No way.

"You're twenty-four, Regina. It's time you settled down and took on the responsibilities of being a Winterborne. You will inherit everything I have worked my entire life to build and that my forefathers worked to build before me. If you're not ready for that challenge, you might lose everything."

Now that grabbed her attention. She looked at her father for the first time since the conversation began. "What do you mean I might *lose* everything?"

He shook his head sadly from side to side. "I had no choice but to make a codicil to my will. Unless I am fully convinced that you are prepared to take over the company and run it properly, the board of directors will run things as per my final instructions and you will receive a monthly allowance until such time that they deem you fit to take charge of the company."

Horror burgeoned like a scream in her throat. "But...but," she croaked, "how will I live?" Begging on a street corner flashed vividly through her mind. Dear God, he couldn't be serious. His idea of an allowance was laughable at best. And those crusty old codgers on the board hated her!

"It doesn't have to come to that," he said pointedly.

"All you have to do is trust me and you'll have *everything.*"

The horror drained away leaving an almost blinding clarity. "In other words, if I marry this Texan I get everything...if I don't I get a measly allowance."

Indignation washed across her father's pale, pudgy face. "Your allowance has never been measly!" The red started to rise up his neck once more. Oops! She'd hit a nerve with that one. "You have always, always gotten anything you asked for. I have never permitted you to want for anything." Something in his expression changed and a new kind of fear crept up her spine. "Perhaps," he suggested furiously, "that is part of the problem."

"Daddy," she wailed, suddenly sure of what he intended next, "you can't seriously want me to marry a man I've never even met!" Even *she* wasn't that impetuous.

Her father lifted one shaggy eyebrow in that condescending manner he'd always used with her when he actually wanted to turn her over his knee and spank her. But he never had, not once. "That's precisely why we're spending the weekend at his ranch. We're going to get to know him and that is the end of the subject. If you wish to stay on my good side, you will do as I request."

Do it or lose it, that was the bottom line. She could stay single and play all she wanted if she were willing to give up the fortune that, as the only Winterborne heir, she was fully entitled to. Or she could buckle under and marry some stranger who would probably boss her around just like her father did.

Wow, what a choice.

"I want you packed and ready to go in one hour," he ordered. "I absolutely will not tolerate any grief either, young lady. You will behave yourself this weekend or you will be sorry. Is that clear?"

She stared directly into her father's worried eyes. He loved her. She knew he did. In his mind he was only trying to save her from herself. She didn't doubt for a moment his heart was in the right place, but that didn't make her like it. Then there was the money to consider.

What good would her freedom be if she were perpetually broke?

"Yes, Daddy," she said in the most obedient tone she could muster. "I'll go pack."

The telephone rang and her father hurried over to his desk to answer it. Regina peered out the window once more and tried to picture the bleakness of Texas. She despised long stretches of nothing. She was scared to death of horses. And she absolutely hated macho, arrogant men. How on earth was she supposed to survive on that stupid ranch even for a weekend?

The image of her birthright, billions of dollars, circling the proverbial drain and disappearing flashed in her mind's eye. Okay, maybe she could survive it for just a little while.

"I'll be right there," she heard her father say, his tone urgent. She frowned. Where could he be going when they had to leave in just one hour? Before she could ask that very question, he skirted his desk and rushed over to her.

"The employees at one of the facilities have walked out, shutting down the whole operation. I've got to get over there and see if I can get this worked out. We can't afford any bad publicity of any sort right now."

In other words, her father didn't want the cowboy to find out since it might give him pause.

"Of course," she said, suddenly elated. This meant they didn't have to go to Texas, which bought her a little more time to figure a way out of this. "I'm sure Mr. Calhoun will understand our postponing." She resisted the urge to do a little end-zone victory dance. Hot dog! She was free for the weekend. Fireworks and all-night parties.

"Oh, no," her father said, positively mortified at the very idea. "His private plane is already on its way to pick us up. You go on ahead of me. I'll join the two of you as soon as I have this little misunderstanding worked out." He gave her a pointed look. "Just don't mention anything about it, all right, dear?"

Her hopes fizzled like a dud firecracker. "Fine," she muttered. What else could she do? Her whole future depended on her cooperation. The way she saw it, the only choice she had was to try and figure out a way to send this cowboy running in another direction. If he chose not to marry her, then it certainly wouldn't be her fault.

She smiled. Oh yeah, that could work. And her father wouldn't be the wiser.

"OH, MY GOD," Amy murmured as she stopped midway down the mile-long drive and admired the house that loomed before her. The Winterborne mansion was huge. Not just huge, she amended, palatial. That was it, she decided. It looked like an enormous castle with acres of magnificent gardens flanking it. The only thing missing was the moat.

Amy eased off the brake and rolled the rest of the way up the drive, past the elaborate fountain, choosing to park near the side of the grand house rather than up front. As she emerged from her car she noted that somehow her dilapidated old compact just wouldn't look right at the bottom of those luxurious steps.

Suddenly conscious of her attire, she smoothed a hand over her travel-wrinkled slacks. She straightened her sleeveless sweater and squared her shoulders. She was a courier for the Colby Agency. She might not live in a mansion or drive a Rolls, but this was important business.

Amy marched up the steps and straight to the massive double doors. She pressed the doorbell and waited for a butler to answer. Surely in a house like this, the residents didn't bother answering the door themselves.

The door suddenly swung inward and a young woman, maybe about Amy's age, stared out at her, annoyance written all over her face. "Just a minute," she barked into the cordless phone she clutched in her right hand. "What do you want?" she demanded of Amy.

Taken aback but determined to maintain her professionalism, she dredged up a smile. "Good afternoon, I'm Amy Wells from the Colby Agency. I believe Mr. Winterborne is expecting me."

The woman looked her up and down disapprovingly. To Amy's credit, she didn't squirm. "He's not here. He had to leave. I'll tell him you came by."

Wait a minute. That wasn't going to work. Victoria had said that Mr. Winterborne needed this report right away. "Wait!" Amy cried before the door could slam in her face.

"What?" the woman snapped, obviously in a hurry to get back to whoever was on the other end of the telephone line.

Amy positioned herself in the doorway to prevent its closing. "I have to give this report to Mr. Winterborne. It's very important."

"Fine," the woman relented. "Come in and you can call him at the plant."

Amy stepped into the marble-floored entry hall and was awestruck all over again by the grandness of the home. The outside was beautiful but the inside was breathtaking.

The woman moved a few feet away to resume her call. "I can't believe you're even calling me like this," she hissed.

Amy tried to focus on the details of the amazing entry hall rather than on the hushed words, but the intensity of the phone conversation prodded her natural curiosity.

"No," the woman said sharply. "You walked out on me, Kevin. Left me here to deal with my father."

Now Amy got the picture. The girl was apparently Mr. Winterborne's daughter and the caller, or "callee" as the case might be, was obviously her boyfriend…or ex-boyfriend.

"Vegas? What the hell are you doing in—?"

Silence echoed for about five seconds.

"How much?" This time her fury had dissolved into something like awe. The same kind of awe Amy had felt at seeing this place. "You won that much?"

Okay, Amy reasoned. Her boyfriend was in Vegas and had just won a lot of money and was calling to…make up? Amy grinned. She definitely had this investigating thing down to a science. She just had to find a way to get Victoria's attention. Simply asking for the position wouldn't be good enough. Amy wanted to bowl her employer over with some sort of amazing feat. That way she would just have to say yes! No wouldn't even be a possibility.

"Don't say that unless you mean it," the woman said wistfully.

Amy's heart went out to her. Was this guy trying to win her back? Did he deserve a second chance? Her gut instinct was that anytime a person had a chance at true love, he or she had better take it. It sure didn't come along often.

"Okay," the woman said breathlessly. "I'm going

to the airport right now. I'll be on the next flight out there.'' She giggled. ''Yes. I love you, too.''

Amy had been right all the way around. The thought pleased her immensely.

The woman jumped when her gaze collided with Amy's once more. ''Oh. I'd forgotten all about you.''

Amy kept her smile in place in spite of the indifference radiating from the other woman. ''I just need to deliver this report to your father.''

The woman, who Amy had decided was Miss Winterborne, nodded. ''He's at the Caldwell facility.'' She started for the door. ''I'll give you directions or the number. Whichever you want, but I'm in a hurry here.''

Amy followed, the white envelope clasped in her hand. Victoria's instructions had been for her to deliver it personally to Mr. Winterborne. Driving to another destination wouldn't be a problem as long as she accomplished her mission. ''Directions will be fine.''

Miss Winterborne opened the door, but then quickly closed it. She turned back to Amy, her eyes round with something like horror. ''They're here,'' she said on a breath that rushed out of her lungs as if she'd seen a ghost.

Who was here?

Whoever it was, it was none of Amy's concern. She had a job to do. Failure wasn't an option if she wanted to keep Victoria Colby-Camp impressed. ''You were going to give me directions to—''

''Ah…stay right here.'' Miss Winterborne rushed

to the other end of the long hall and grabbed something. As she hurried back to the door Amy recognized the object as a designer suitcase, the kind that looked like a huge old-fashioned purse and had probably cost more than Amy's monthly salary. "I'll be right back," the woman assured Amy before slipping out the door.

What was going on here? Amy suddenly remembered the telephone conversation and how Miss Winterborne had promised to get the next flight...

Surely she wasn't leaving Amy here to fend for herself. She glanced around the enormous hall. The house seemed empty. How would she find out where Mr. Winterborne was if the daughter disappeared on her?

She couldn't.

And that was unacceptable.

Amy jerked open the front door and strode out onto the landing that topped the dozen half-moon steps which descended to the U-shaped drive.

A long black limousine sat at the bottom of the steps. A driver placed the bag Miss Winterborne had exited the house with into the trunk and closed the lid. He smiled at Amy and quickly hurried around to the driver's door.

Where was Regina Winterborne?

Amy looked left then right but saw no sign of her. Her gaze went straight to the tinted windows then. She must already be inside the car. Annoyed, Amy charged down the steps intent on demanding to know where Mr. Winterborne was.

"Good afternoon, Miss Winterborne," a male voice

said bringing her up short two steps shy of the car. "I'm Mr. Beckman."

Amy whipped around expecting to see the woman right behind her somehow, instead the only thing she found was a tall, well-dressed gentleman smiling down at her.

"Where's—"

Before Amy could complete her question, the man gestured to the car's passenger-side door. "The plane is waiting. Mr. Winterborne already informed us that he would arrive later in the weekend."

The plane? What plane?

Amy shook her head, confusion bearing down on her now. Where was the woman? Regina Winterborne? Amy had to deliver this report. "I'm supposed—"

"We're behind schedule as it is," the man said, his tone direct. He moved past her and opened the door. "We don't want to keep Mr. Calhoun waiting."

Mr. Calhoun? Who…?

The image of the man astride the horse immediately flashed in her brain. The guy in the report. She looked down at the white envelope. Mr. Winterborne's report.

"The flight will take about three hours but the bar is fully stocked and you can watch a movie if you'd like." He grasped her arm firmly and urged her toward the open door. "We have several to choose from."

Wait a minute! Realization belatedly sank through the fog of confusion. He'd called *her* Miss Winterborne.

"But I'm not—"

Mr. Beckman smiled patiently. "I'm sure you will be by the time this weekend has concluded. Mr. Calhoun is quite the charmer."

With that said, he promptly hoisted her into the car and closed the door. Before she could even blink he slid into the seat next to the driver and ordered, "Let's go."

Just when Amy would have roared her indignation something caught her eye…or, actually, the lack of something. Her car was gone. She whipped around in the seat as the limo circled the fountain and headed down the long drive. It was gone all right. She'd left the keys in the ignition since she'd only expected to deliver the report at the door, not go inside. Who would have expected it to be stolen here of all places?

And then she knew.

The woman—Miss Winterborne—had stolen it. To go to the airport to catch a flight to Vegas where she would rendezvous with her boyfriend.

Shaking her head, Amy turned around and moved to the edge of her seat. "Look," she said to the two men in the front seat, "there's been a big mistake."

The one named Beckman glanced over his shoulder at her. "Everything will be fine, Miss Winterborne," he said again in that patient, practiced tone. "Just relax and this will go a lot more smoothly."

What would go a lot more smoothly? Anger jolted Amy. Dammit, why wouldn't the man listen to her? "I'm trying to tell you that I'm not—"

Before she could finish her statement the privacy window powered up between the passenger compartment and the front seat, leaving her talking to herself.

Fury exploding in her like an erupting volcano, she pounded on the tinted glass that separated her from the only other two people in the vehicle. "You've got the wrong girl," she shouted for the good it would do with the privacy glass up, making the passenger compartment not only invisible to them but also soundproof. She tried the door handle but it was locked. Not that it would have done her any good anyway. People might jump out of moving cars all the time in the movies but she certainly had no desire to.

Okay. She eased back in the seat and took a breath. He'd said the plane was waiting which meant they were headed to an airport. Once there they would have to let her out of the car to board the plane. She would explain then that she wasn't who they thought she was.

She fumed at the idea that the real Miss Winterborne had stolen her car. Fear momentarily paralyzed Amy. What if Miss Winterborne was in some sort of trouble and had left Amy to take the heat for her?

Beckman could be some kind of loan shark or…her eyes widened in fear when she considered the numerous other possibilities.

Then she remembered that he'd mentioned Mr. Calhoun. Amy relaxed marginally. Mr. Calhoun was waiting, so they were obviously headed to meet him. Amy's eyes widened once more. Calhoun lived in Texas.

She snatched up the envelope and pulled out the report on the man. She'd skimmed it while she fueled up and hadn't noticed anything negative. Maybe she'd better read it more carefully. Men who were on the up and up surely didn't send the hired help to collect a woman against her will. Had Regina Winterborne wanted to take this trip she wouldn't have run off after her ex in Vegas. Amy steamed when she thought about how Beckman had all but shoved her into the car and then locked her inside.

No wonder the real Miss Winterborne had run away.

Amy's eyes rounded again. What if her father and this Mr. Calhoun had made some sort of deal that Miss Winterborne was trying to escape?

What if she knew something terrible about the man and feared for her safety?

Amy's gaze landed on the report once more. If John Robert Calhoun, IV, had anything to hide, she was certain the Colby Agency would have found it. All Amy needed to do was scour these pages and then maybe—just maybe—she could save Miss Winterborne from whatever fate lay in store for her in Texas. Surely Miss Winterborne's father wouldn't send her to a man who was anything less than honorable.

Another realization struck Amy then. Mr. Winterborne hadn't seen the report. He had no idea what kind of man Calhoun really was. By the time this car reached the airport Amy had every intention of knowing all there was to know about John Robert Calhoun, IV.

VICTORIA SURVEYED her desk once more. She never misplaced notes. Never.

"Mildred," she said to her longtime secretary who

waited patiently nearby, "I'm sorry, but I seem to have lost them."

"That's all right. I can bring you a copy of the one I made for the file after Trent dictated the information to me."

Victoria nodded absently. This simply wasn't like her. She never lost anything, certainly not something as important as preliminary notes on an ongoing case.

"Thank you, Mildred. I'll try not to lose this one."

Mildred went off to make the new copy and Victoria huffed her impatience. Thank goodness the notes hadn't mentioned anyone by name, only the negative activity that Trent Tucker, one of her best investigators in the art of tracking and surveillance, had discovered. If the notes had accidentally ended up in the trash, rather than being filed or placed in the burn bag for destruction, at least no one would know to whom the illegal activities were connected.

The Colby Agency prided itself on discretion.

Victoria sighed wearily. It was Friday and it was late. She should go home and put work out of her mind. Everyone else, except Mildred, of course, had already left for the day in anticipation of the holiday weekend.

She might as well do the same.

Lucas didn't want her putting in too many hours at the office just yet.

Warmth welled in her chest.

It was nice having someone to worry about her.

There was absolutely no reason for her to worry about anything except sharing a holiday weekend with her husband and son. Her family.

All else would take care of itself.

Chapter Three

This was bad.

Amy stared at the words on the final page of the Calhoun report. On the surface this guy appeared to be above reproach, but behind the perfect facade lurked incredible evil.

She shivered as she read the words once more. Calhoun was suspected of having ties to the mob and would apparently do almost anything to make money. Amy frowned and shuffled the pages once more. The entire report was squeaky clean except for this one page. At first she'd thought maybe this page didn't even go with the report, but then she'd read in there somewhere that any additional information discovered would be attached. Well, this was definitely additional information even if unconfirmed. Trent Tucker was working on confirmation at this very moment.

Amy chewed her thumbnail. It was downright awful. Mr. Winterborne certainly wouldn't have sent his one and only daughter off for the weekend at Mr. Calhoun's had he suspected any of this. Amy was certain of that, though she was still irritated at the woman's audacity. She'd stolen Amy's car and taken off, leaving her to face this mess. But then again, she was trained for this sort of situation. She knew how to handle herself, physically and emotionally.

Amy stilled. Maybe this was her chance to prove her worth as an investigator. She could ferret out the truth over the weekend. Lord knew she didn't have anything else to do. Right now all the agency had was suspicions. But she could find the connection, she was sure of it. She would have access to Calhoun's home…to his private files maybe.

A smile spread across her lips as anticipation rushed through her. This could be her first case, even if she had come by it unexpectedly. Beckman had said that Mr. Winterborne wouldn't be joining them right away and neither he nor the driver appeared to realize that she was not Regina Winterborne. If that held true with Calhoun, Amy would have some time, maybe even the whole weekend, to covertly investigate the man.

The smile turned into an outright grin. Oh yeah. This was the moment she'd been waiting for. If she could make the connection, turn suspicion into fact, then she would have proven not only her ability but her value as an investigator.

All she had to do was play along with this little game of mistaken identity. That Mr. Calhoun was gorgeous amounted to mere icing on the cake. God had finally answered her prayers.

It was fate.

That's all it could be.

The limo braked to a stop at a private airfield and Amy allowed Beckman to escort her to the Learjet standing by. She supposed that it wasn't outside the realm of possibility that Calhoun would have a private jet. He was, after all, an oil tycoon. So she wouldn't count that against him, but such pretentiousness definitely set her instincts on point. Though she didn't know any men who owned a jet, she could imagine arrogance went along with that kind of presumed self-importance. Well, she had news for Mr. Calhoun: the bigger they are, the harder they fall.

His secrets were about to be revealed.

There were a number of other things about him she'd like to have revealed, but the job came first. She shivered at the thought of his picture.

Amy utilized the flight time to recall everything she'd ever heard about the Winterbornes. She didn't know that much but she felt as though she had enough information to fake it. If—very big if—Calhoun had not met Regina as she suspected, pulling off this charade would be easy. But she wouldn't know until she got there…unless…

She decided to go for broke.

"Does Mr. Calhoun prefer to be called John or Robert?" she asked of Beckman who appeared immersed in the files he'd brought along in his briefcase. She wasn't the only one who'd decided to make this a working flight, she mused.

Beckman looked up at her over his wire-rimmed glasses. "John," he said after studying her for a moment. "He prefers to be called John."

Amy nodded, not certain whether that was a positive response or a negative one. She still didn't know for sure if Regina had met him. For some reason Beckman looked at her suspiciously now. Had she blown it already? Her pulse tripped into overtime.

Putting his files aside, Beckman leveled his gaze on her. "Miss Winterborne, John is an honorable man. He doesn't expect this to be easy at first. But, in the long run, it is the right thing to do for both of you."

Amy had a bad feeling about the "it" he referred to. It was her understanding that Mr. Winterborne intended a business deal with Mr. Calhoun and hoped his daughter would like the man, which would facilitate future business dealings. Maybe she was wrong about that.

"I'm not sure what you mean," she said as vaguely as possible with her heart pounding. That bad feeling had morphed into something resembling fear. Call it intuition, call it ESP, but Amy was suddenly certain this whole charade might just be a really bad idea.

"Why, a marriage between you and John, what else?" Beckman said as if she should have known precisely what he meant.

Marriage?

"You really expect Re—" Amy caught herself just in time "—me to marry a man I don't even know?" Well, there. She'd said it plainly enough. If Regina had, in fact, met John before, Amy's cover was blown completely.

A kind of haughtiness that bordered on ugly flickered in Beckman's eyes. "Let's be honest here," he said, his tone matching his hateful expression. "It's not as if you're some naive little maiden now, is it? As I understand it, you've made quite a reputation for yourself among the rich bachelors in the Chicago area. I'd say this is your one chance to redeem yourself."

Fury boiled up inside Amy. Fury for Regina Winterborne. How dare this man speak so harshly about her when the woman wasn't even here to defend herself.

But then...he didn't know that.

Well, she'd just have to do the defending.

"I beg your pardon," Amy retorted, allowing him to hear and see the depth of her indignation.

Beckman smirked. "Come on, Miss Winterborne, I've heard all about your exploits. The last one...what was his name?" Beckman stroked his chin thoughtfully. "Ah yes, Kevin something-or-other. He helped you go through a few hundred thousand of your daddy's money and then he disappeared. Does that about sum up your most recent relationship?"

Kevin...that was the name of the guy Regina had been speaking with when Amy arrived. She was running off to meet him at that very moment. In Vegas no less. Amy blinked, momentarily disconcerted. Should she just tell Beckman the truth here and now? What if she were wrong? What if Calhoun was all that he appeared to be and Regina was the wacky one? What if Amy had this thing all wrong?

Then she remembered the suspicions in the report. Suspicions that amounted to far worse than having a fling and running through a little money with a scum-bag boyfriend.

Amy leaned forward, putting herself several inches closer to the condescending jerk who'd dragged her into this mess. "Mr. Beckman, you have no idea who I am. That you would judge me on such hearsay is appalling. Perhaps I should take up the issue with Mr. Calhoun when we arrive."

Beckman's smirk wilted instantly. "That won't be necessary, Miss Winterborne. I'm certain you're right." He squirmed a bit more before he added, "You surely understand that Mr. Calhoun's well-being is my only concern in the matter. I simply would hate to see his heart broken."

Amy doubted his sincerity but let it go at that. Besides, she was pretty sure Mr. John Robert Calhoun, IV, could take care of himself. He certainly looked man enough. Another shiver swept over her skin. In fact, she imagined he could take care of most anything. Like a toe-curling, full-body orgasm. The kind magazines raved about all the time. The kind she'd never had. What was she saying? She hadn't had one, period, in about two years. Work, she reminded herself. She was too busy for a personal life.

John Calhoun, IV, would be about work. No matter how good-looking, no matter how seemingly perfect, she would not be swayed from her ultimate goal. Cracking his apparently impervious veneer and revealing the fraud behind it would certainly test her ability. Would show once and for all that she was agent material. Amy had faith in herself. She'd wanted this opportunity for far too long to allow anything to stop her. Not for love nor money would she be deterred.

Mr. Calhoun had better be on his toes because Amy Wells was onto him.

JOHN JERKED his string tie loose once more and muttered a curse. Why the hell did it matter what he looked like? This weekend wasn't about what he looked like or even what he wanted in life, it was about closing the deal his father had worked half a lifetime to bring to fruition.

He should just greet the woman naked and let her see all there was to see. She was, if the powers that be had their way, going to be his wife. Why bother with a courtship ritual? It wasn't like any of it mattered?

This was a business merger. One he wasn't fool enough to not see the benefits of, but one he didn't have to like.

John had dated extensively, had had his share of physical relationships. But he'd always assumed that when he settled down for the long haul it would be with a woman who would love him for the man he was, not for the oil business he operated.

That wasn't going to happen. Love, trust, neither of those ingredients would enter into the negotiations. He tugged the tie into a bow once more. Hell, why bother with any of these pretenses? Why not just call over the justice of the peace and have the ceremony performed this very weekend? No point in dragging out the inevitable. All that would do was prolong the agony.

John had never been a glutton for punishment. But he would have more than a wife in name only. That was the one thing he had to make clear this weekend. Infidelity was not his style and he refused to be forced down to that level for sexual gratification. If they were to be married, he would have her in his bed… willingly.

Though he had never met Regina Winterborne, the one photograph he'd seen when his father shoved it in front of his face promised an attractive woman. Her dark hair had been up in a ponytail and equally dark glasses had shielded her eyes, but she'd looked appealing otherwise even if the photograph had appeared to have caught her off guard. He had to ask himself, however, why a woman like that would allow herself to be manipulated into a loveless marriage?

For the same reasons he allowed it, John supposed.

He was the only heir, as she was. Their fathers obviously had their futures plotted out to the best interest of their respective companies. John wasn't oblivious to the long-term benefits. But, dammit, this was the twenty-first century. Arranged marriages were a thing of the past. Offspring didn't go to these kinds of extremes anymore to please their parents.

Well, he admitted, most didn't, anyhow.

But here he was, primping to meet the woman he was supposed to marry in order to facilitate a business merger.

"You've lost your mind," he said to his reflection in the full-length mirror.

He wouldn't go back on his word. That was a given. John never broke a promise. He would see this weekend through and, if possible, he would come to an agreement with the woman. But he would have to know that there was hope for something more. That was the one promise he made to himself.

He would spend this weekend getting to know Regina Winterborne and, when it was over, if there was even a hint of hope, he would take the next step. But first he had to know that falling in love was at least a possibility. It wouldn't take long to make that determination. He had three days and three nights. She would leave on Monday afternoon. The fact that her father probably wouldn't be able to join them until around noon on Sunday was all the better. He needed time with the woman alone. Without interference from anyone else, including Nate. John intended to send him on his way as well. This had to be between John Calhoun and Regina Winterborne.

By the time their seventy-two hours together were up, he would know if she was the kind of woman with whom he could spend the rest of his life...to whom he could give his heart.

As sentimental as it sounded, that was the bottom line for John. Though his mother had been dead for more than a decade now, he still remembered the way his father had looked at her. The way she had looked at his father. That was what he wanted. Admittedly, under the circumstances, he might have to wait for it.

But he had to have some promise that it could be forthcoming.

Anything less was unacceptable.

A light knock on his bedroom door dragged John from his troubling musings.

"It's open."

The door eased away from the frame and Liam stuck his head inside the room. "They're here," he said in his usual annoyed tone. Liam had worked on the Wild Horse for as long as John could remember and he hated when his normal routine was disrupted. "Nate called in and said they'd just turned onto Stampede Lane."

"Thanks, Liam," John said, mustering a smile for the old man.

He grumbled something resembling a "you're welcome" and shut the door.

John took a last look at himself. His jeans were clean and freshly starched, as was his white shirt. The black string tie and freshly polished boots finished off the getup. Good enough for church, good enough for this, he decided. Anything more than that would have been too much. He had no intention of going out of his way until he saw further. Until he knew *she* was worth the extra exertion.

That was callous, he railed silently. But this was enough to make any man callous.

Settling his Stetson into place, John descended the stairs and opted to wait in the long entry hall that welcomed visitors to his family home. Stampede Lane was actually the driveway to the property, but it extended three miles so he had another moment or two.

He glanced around the room and wondered what a city dweller would think of his home. Not that he really cared. He'd loved this home his whole life. His mother had designed it and, as far as John was concerned, the southwestern villa was the most beautiful place in north Texas. If Miss Regina Winterborne didn't like it, well that was her problem because this was where they would live.

His father had moved into a retirement community nearly three years ago. Not because John wanted him to, by God. He'd tried everything to talk his father into staying. But the stubborn old man had insisted that moving was what he wanted. Shortly after settling into the small but luxurious apartment community, John had realized why. J. R. Calhoun, as he was known to his friends, was in hog heaven. There were at least ten retired widows living in the community to every one retired widower. J.R. spent five nights out of seven having dinner with one available female or the other.

He did reserve Sunday nights for his one and only son. And Friday nights were for poker and catching his breath, he laughingly told John.

John really couldn't blame him. His father had been incredibly lonesome since his wife of nearly forty years had died. John had the ranch as well as the business under control. What was there for him to do, J.R. had insisted? And he'd been right. He might as well enjoy his final days on this earth in whatever fashion he chose.

But John had a feeling that rugged old bucks like his father lived forever. Or, at the very least, long enough to see that his only son's life was charted out just the way he wanted it.

John squared his shoulders and pushed the thoughts away. He had to stay focused this weekend. He had just seventy-two hours to determine if he could spend the rest of his life with Regina Winterborne.

AMY TRIED to stifle a gasp but failed miserably as the car parked in front of the house belonging to John Calhoun.

Mr. Beckman glanced at her, clearly surprised by her reaction.

The Calhoun home was no more ostentatious than the Winterborne place. But there was something more personal about it. Like the Winterborne mansion, the house was very large. But rather than a castle-like structure, this was a southwestern-style villa, complete with a red-tiled roof. Serving as a lush backdrop were north Texas's vivid green pastures dappled with clusters of trees and horses. Acres and acres of white rail fencing closed in the pastures that went on for as far as the eye could see. The infinite beauty was interrupted only by the occasional barn.

There were no meticulous gardens as there had been at the Winterborne estate, but the grounds were nicely landscaped just the same. A couple of four-wheel-drive, crew-cab trucks sat near the house, and there was not a luxury automobile in sight. The limo that had brought them from the airport to the ranch was a rental, as had been the one back in Chicago.

Mr. Beckman opened the car door and gestured for Amy to get out first. He had chosen to sit in the passenger compartment with her on this leg of the journey. She'd at first thought he had grown suspicious of her since she'd asked so many questions, but he'd seemed completely at ease as the miles had rolled out behind them.

"Welcome to the Wild Horse Ranch," he said as he emerged from the limo to stand beside her. "I'm sure you'll find your stay here a pleasant one."

Amy turned around slowly so that she could take in every detail without the obstruction of tinted glass. It was even more beautiful than she'd first thought. Even a city girl like her could appreciate the sheer natural splendor of it.

"It's not what I expected," she admitted, certain that Regina Winterborne would have said the same thing.

Beckman smiled. "Most people react that way when they first visit." He escorted her up the walk while the driver removed the bag from the trunk. It was the first time Amy had thought about clothes. She sure hoped she and Regina wore the same size. As she recalled, the young woman who'd left her in this predicament looked about the same size as her.

"I'll be going back into town once I've made the formal introductions," Beckman explained, breaking into her wardrobe worries.

For the first time since this adventure began, Amy

felt an inkling of uncertainty. "You won't be staying?" That could mean that she and John Calhoun would be alone. Then again, she didn't really like Beckman, why did she care if he left?

Because at least she knew him. She stopped on the portico and stared at the massive door that led into the enormous home. What lay beyond that intricately carved wooden door was the unknown. A man who had secrets…dirty secrets if the suspicions she'd read panned out. Secrets she wanted to reveal in order to thwart whatever evil plan he had in store for poor, unsuspecting Regina Winterborne. To do that she had to step through that door and stick to the ruse she'd been dragged into and ultimately decided to use to her advantage.

The only down side was that she was on her own.

What had felt like the perfect plan now seemed foolish and shortsighted.

But what could she do? She was here. This man thought she was Regina Winterborne. What choice did she have but to see this through?

None.

If she ever wanted to be a Colby agent, she had to prove her worth. Not to mention that if she blew it now without getting the goods on Calhoun, she'd have a heck of a time convincing Victoria that she hadn't jumped in over her head.

Sadly though, Amy feared that she had done just that.

The door suddenly opened wide and the cowboy she had admired in the photograph stood before her.

He was taller than she'd imagined. His shoulders were even wider than she'd guessed. But the one asset to which the photograph had truly failed to do justice was the eyes. They were the bluest she'd ever seen. Piercing, startling blue. And right that second they were focused fully on her.

"Welcome to the Wild Horse, ma'am," the cowboy said in a deep, husky voice that sent goose bumps skittering across her skin.

"Th-thank you," she stuttered in time with the stumbling of her heart. My God, the way he said *ma'am* gave her goose bumps.

"Miss Winterborne," Beckman cut in, startling Amy all over again since she'd completely forgotten his presence, "this is John Calhoun. John, this is Regina Winterborne."

"Come in." The cowboy looked from her to Beckman. "Both of you."

With that Amy was led into his home. Her breath caught again as her gaze traveled over the cathedral ceiling with its massive wooden beams, and the white-washed stucco walls, and on to the terra-cotta-tiled floor.

Except for a leather sofa, the furniture clustered about the room consisted mostly of wooden pieces and all of it was dark and polished to a high sheen. Plaid and striped throw pillows accented the butter-soft leather of the sofa and proud wingback chairs.

But nothing in the entry hall or the enormous great room into which he led her took away from the real mind blower—the man. If Amy had ever laid eyes on a more gorgeous specimen of the male species she had no recall of it now.

John Robert Calhoun, IV, was definitely the perfect man.

Her gaze collided with his and she didn't miss the same approval mirrored there. Judging by what she noted in his eyes he liked what he saw as well. Heat kindled low in her belly and her heart fluttered, but then suddenly sank like rock in a freshwater pond as did her smile. John Calhoun thought he was looking into the eyes of his future wife. And he liked what he saw.

Too bad she was just a stand-in—one who intended to uncover all his well-hidden secrets.

That goal suddenly felt all wrong.

But it was too late to back out now.

The game had already begun.

Chapter Four

She wasn't what he'd expected.

It was true that John had only seen the one picture of Regina Winterborne and in it she'd worn dark glasses. The long, silky dark hair he'd anticipated. The petite frame softened by slight feminine curves he'd noted in the photo. But it was the sheer innocence and vulnerability in her eyes that startled him. That calf-caught-in-the-fence look of fear.

Surely a woman as experienced with the opposite sex as Regina Winterborne wasn't afraid of him…

Marriage.

The epiphany kicked him in the gut with all the force of an ornery mule.

It wasn't him she was afraid of…it was the idea of commitment. The new rules and boundaries she no doubt realized would rule her world.

John glanced at Nate who looked past ready to get this show on the road. Had he relayed John's non-negotiable terms already? Dread knotted in his gut. He didn't want this weekend to start off on the wrong foot, especially considering old man Winterborne wouldn't be here to serve as a buffer. But John would be damned if he'd change his mind.

If he was required to take a wife to seal this deal, then she would be more than an in-name-only accessory. Their relationship would be the real thing.

John tensed as those lovely brown eyes swept down the length of him, then bounced back up to meet his. He'd have to have been blind to miss the startled amazement and undeniable approval reflected there. Miss Winterborne liked what she saw. Unexpectedly a flick of heat slid through him, making him tingle. Maybe this could work after all. It had been a long time since a woman, one he'd only just met, made him tingle. Were his father here, he'd insist that it wouldn't be that way if John didn't keep himself busy all the time with those danged horses.

His father was of the mindset that running one of the country's largest oil businesses was enough stress for any man. He didn't believe his son needed to take on the added pressure of single-handedly attempting to save the wild equines that roamed the few unpopulated territories of the West. But John knew what he had to do…recognized his calling. Nothing his father said was going to change that.

Neither was the woman standing in front of him right now. His gaze raked her lean but feminine body once more. The low-riding slacks, funky belt and sweater that offered a little glimpse of flat belly appealed to him, that was for sure. But nothing would change his mind. She'd either accept his world for what it was or she could go back to Chicago and find herself another of those city slickers she appeared to prefer. Well, if all he'd heard was true anyway.

"Perhaps we could all have a drink," Nate suggested, cutting into the thick tension.

John started at the sound of the other man's voice and quickly shook off the irritation welling inside him. He had to get hold of himself here. It was only fair that he give Regina Winterborne the benefit of the doubt. And this weekend was far too important for him to go jumping the gun. There were assessments to make, and concessions too, most likely. He glanced at his wife-to-be once more. If her self-serving reputation proved true, which he suspected it would, since her own daddy had bemoaned her impetuousness as well as her petulance, she would want her own way on some things. Most things probably. Only time would tell if her way and John's would mesh.

"That's a mighty fine idea, Nate," John said. A good, stiff drink was something he imagined both he and Miss Winterborne could use right about now. If memory served she preferred some sissy wine that Liam had special-ordered for this visit.

"What's your pleasure, Miss Winterborne?" Nate asked their guest.

She blinked a couple of times. "I'll have whatever you gentlemen are having," she replied, her voice a little too high, her expression flustered.

John tamped down the need to frown. Liam had

ordered that fancy white wine just for her. Maybe he should tell her that her preferred drink was available. Her daddy had said she drank nothing else. The frown nudged its way onto his brow. Then again, daddies didn't always know what their little girls liked best. Deciding the idea merited no further contemplation, he gestured to the couch and suggested, "Make yourself comfortable, Miss Winterborne."

"You have a beautiful home, Mr. Calhoun," she said a little breathlessly as she turned around slowly to admire the room once more before taking a seat.

He tried to see the place as she would. He'd grown up in this house. Had personally overseen the latest remodeling three years ago. Somehow he'd managed to keep the scheme of things the way his mother had intended. He definitely hadn't wanted to change that. It made him feel close to her. Damn. Even after a dozen years he still missed her.

"Call me John," he said to the lady now perched stiffly on one end of his leather couch. He settled into one of the matching wing chairs. The soft, supple brown leather furnishings had replaced the old plaid jobs that had served his family in this room for as long as he could remember. But time and the rambunctious kid he'd been had long ago worn out the comfortable old pieces. Even the frames had been beyond repair leaving him no alternative but to replace everything. He'd picked out the new furniture himself. He wondered briefly if his guest liked his taste. This would be her home as well, after all.

She smiled and something shifted in his chest at the sweetness, the utter genuineness of the expression. "If we're going to be on a first-name basis," she ventured timidly, "I suppose you should call me…" She swallowed, looking suddenly ill at ease once more.

"Do you prefer Regina or Gina?" he asked when she clamped down on her lower lip in uncertainty.

"Gina," she said in a rush, relief flooding her expression.

This was one nervous little filly, he decided. "Gina it is then."

Nate returned with three tumblers of Scotch. "Gina," he said as he offered a glass to her. He'd obviously heard her response to John's question, which wasn't surprising since the man missed nothing. "Enjoy."

"Thank you." She took the glass and held it gingerly.

Frowning, John took his own tumbler. "Thanks, Nate."

Nate flashed one of his famous smiles and John considered for the thousandth time that the man had missed his calling. He should be running for political office.

"To the future," Nate offered as he held up his glass.

"The future," John echoed, his gaze landing on his guest as she glanced uneasily at the drink in her hand. He watched her over the rim of his glass as he drank deeply of the amber liquor. She grimaced at the first touch of liquor to her lips.

"If you'd prefer wine," Nate hastened to say, obviously noting her reaction as well.

"No. This is fine," she squeaked, then cleared her throat and took another tiny swallow.

To her credit she didn't grimace this time but the shine in her eyes told John she'd paid dearly for holding it back. That annoying frown nagged at his forehead again. Something wasn't right here, but he couldn't say just what yet. Only one thing was certain, she needed rescuing at the moment.

John set his glass aside and stood. "Why don't I show you to your room?" He smiled as warmly as he could manage with her looking scared half to death. "I'm sure you'd like some time to catch your breath before dinner."

She nodded jerkily and scrambled to her feet. "That would be really nice."

"I'll be on my way then," Nate said as he stood. "Since Mr. Winterborne was unable to make it, I'm serving as your father's card-playing partner," he said to John.

John only nodded, but Gina looked stricken.

"When will you be back?" she asked faintly.

"I'll check in with you tomorrow." He smiled. "Good evening." Then he disappeared, leaving the two of them standing there in awkward silence.

"This way," John finally said.

She followed him up the stairs without saying a

word, as if he were leading her to the gallows. He got the distinct impression that Miss Winterborne liked this whole situation about as much as he did. Or maybe less, he decided when he paused at the door of the guest room to which her bag had already been delivered.

She looked absolutely mortified. As if he'd just told her to jump out of a plane with no chute.

"You'll find your bag inside." He indicated the closed door. "Dinner is at six."

Amy managed a stiff nod then almost passed out with relief when he turned and walked away.

When he'd disappeared down the stairs, she faced the door of her room. She grasped the knob but closed her eyes and said a little prayer before turning it. *Please don't let this be his room.*

She had no idea how he'd planned to kick off this weekend of getting to know each other before the wedding, but she hoped it wasn't with sex. As amazing as she felt certain it would be, she just couldn't go there…or could she?

Amy stilled as warmth spread through her in spite of her best intentions. He was gorgeous. There was no denying that. But she was here to look into his shady business dealings, not to wind up in his bed.

She imagined, however, that he had altogether different intentions. He, after all, was getting to know his future wife.

Shivering from equal parts of dread and desire, Amy opened the door and entered the room.

Her breath departed her lungs in one long whoosh. The room was large and airy. Floor-to-ceiling windows lined a northern wall allowing in the beautiful light of the Texas sun without permitting the heat a western exposure would have generated. A massive four-poster bed stood against the wall to the left while matching pieces, an armoire, dresser and mirror, dominated the right side of the room. An open door led to a lovely en suite bath and a nearby door opened to a wide inviting closet.

An empty closet, she noted thankfully.

Judging by the empty closet and the well-appointed bathroom that included numerous amenities not unlike those in a luxurious hotel, this was a guest room. Relief flooded her so swiftly that she had to hang on to a bed post to keep her legs under her. The bag Regina Winterborne had packed sat in the middle of the enormous bed.

Amy dragged in a deep breath and gathered her wits. She had to pull herself together here or she'd never be able to accomplish her mission. For the weekend, at least until Sunday, she was Regina Winterborne. She had to do whatever was necessary to keep John Calhoun preoccupied while she uncovered the truth about him and his business dealings. It was a simple matter really, she told herself. Clearly he liked her, would want to learn all he could since she was supposed to be his future wife. That would prove to Amy's advantage. That he called her Gina made her feel a tad better about the whole farce. It felt like less of a lie.

Propelling her weak-kneed legs into action, she climbed onto the bed and opened the criminally expensive bag that held her only wardrobe for the weekend.

A little black dress. Amy checked the size, it would do. But the dress looked entirely too short. She found taupe slacks and a matching sleeveless sweater next. Then she dragged out summery green slacks and a striped blouse. A sound of approval rumbled in her throat. The blouse, tank top in style and with narrow stripes of the same pale green as the pants, white and creamy cantaloupe, looked soft and feminine. Very nice. A peach-colored skirt and matching sleeveless pullover. Another short, form-fitting dress, this one in deep jade. One last slacks outfit and then the coup de grace: a semi-formal-length gown with a halter-style top that plunged low in the back. It was a frosty white with a pencil skirt. Walking would be no easy feat in this dress. Much less in the two pairs of high-spike-heeled shoes that accompanied the wardrobe, one pair in black, the other in white.

Thankfully she saw that a pair of tan-and-white sandals with comfortable flat heels and lovely beading had been packed as well.

Amy's breath caught when she opened the accompanying lingerie bag she'd found next to the shoes. Several thongs with matching barely there bras along with spaghetti-strapped negligées that Amy would never in a million years have been caught in. She held up one lacy white thong and wondered how in the world she would survive wearing something so skimpy, so uncomfortable looking. She tossed it aside and checked out the small cosmetics bag. Lord, the woman carried enough makeup and body scents to start her own line.

She exhaled a heavy sigh. No wonder Amy hadn't had any luck snagging a man. She obviously had no clue how to arm herself. Maybe that magazine was right, maybe she needed lessons on manhunting as well.

For now, if she was going to pretend to be Regina Winterborne she had to dress the part. Amy considered the little black dress and then the jade one. She decided the jade garment was the lesser of the two evils. The neckline was more conservative and the material not quite so clingy as the black. She eyed the shoes skeptically. The sandals wouldn't do, even she had to admit that. That left her no choice but to wear the mile-high black heels. She'd have to practice walking in those things before she went downstairs.

At the moment though, a hot bath was calling her name.

Amy quickly put away her wardrobe for the weekend and ran herself a deep, hot bath. The tub was equipped with whirlpool jets and she couldn't wait to sink into it. Whoever had updated the house last had done an outstanding job from the decorating and furnishings all the way down to the functional elements.

Then again, when one had money one could have almost anything else one desired. Another of those delicious shivers raced through her at the thought of her host. So this was what it was like to have it all....

As Amy sank into the enveloping warmth of the lightly scented water she decided that she would give John Calhoun the benefit of the doubt and assume that he was innocent until she'd proven otherwise. Any court of law would give him that.

She inhaled deeply of the sweet but subtle scent of roses and sighed contentedly. Regina Winterborne's taste in perfumes was not so great in Amy's opinion, but her selection of bath oils was splendid. The lightly scented water would provide all the fragrance she needed. She'd never been one to wear the heavier colognes. This would be just enough.

Closing her eyes, Amy allowed the image of John Calhoun, IV, to invade her weary mind. She was very nearly certain that the magazine designation of the perfect man had been based solely on him. He was absolutely perfect. And those eyes. She smiled and her heart did a breath-stealing little hip-hop. The man had great eyes. His blond hair was thick and she would bet it always had that windblown look about it. Some guys just had naturally great hair and John was one of them. His voice was nice, too. Deep, intoxicating. She shivered again as she recalled the incredibly sexy sound.

Then she wondered if this was what it was like to

be a Colby agent. Glamorous, sexy and so very exciting.

If so, this was definitely the career for her.

JOHN HAD TALKED his father out of coming by tonight. Just barely. The man was like a dog with a bone. He just wouldn't let go until he knew the job was done. He intended to see that John and Gina got off to a good start. Insisting any such visit would make him late for his card game had convinced the stubborn old man in the end. John had a plan of his own. Since Edgar Winterborne wasn't around, he didn't need J. R. Calhoun running interference either.

What John needed was a clear picture of Gina Winterborne. He would only get that if they were alone. Nate had happily agreed to disappear for the entire weekend with only the occasional call to check in. As far as John could see, he was clear until Sunday afternoon when Edgar arrived.

He had close to forty-eight hours to get to know this woman. To decide if he could actually live with this merger.

Knocking back the last of the Scotch in his glass, he set it aside and paced the room once more, as he had for the past hour. There was a definite physical attraction, he admitted. She was a good-looking woman, soft and feminine. That part hadn't surprised him. What had caught him completely off guard was the sweetness that seemed so out of character with what he'd read about her past.

He wondered vaguely if her wild past had been exaggerated. But that didn't make sense since her own father had admitted to her unabashed behavior. Regina Winterborne, Gina, had a reputation for being bad and loving it. The woman—John glanced toward the stairs—currently taking up space in his guest room didn't seem like the type at all.

But looks could be deceiving, which made him wonder all over again if he could trust anything she said. What if all this sweetness and vulnerability were just an act? What if she won him over in the next forty-eight hours only to make him sorry during the next forty-eight years?

Just then she descended the stairs. The sound of her steps on the treads drew his attention. The oxygen evaporated in his lungs and his jaw dropped to his chest.

She wore a dress the color of emeralds and it hugged the swells and curves of her body like a tailored glove. Long, toned legs went on forever. All that silky brown hair had been arranged into some sort of lush twist or bun on her head, leaving that lovely face and that long slender neck fully exposed for his visual pleasure.

Every muscle in his body went rock-hard. One thing was a certainty right then and there. He could, without reservation, look at this woman for the rest of his life.

"I hope I'm not late," she said softly with a quick glance at the antique clock that rested on the mantle of his stacked stone fireplace.

She was…late that is. But he couldn't care less. He just wanted to keep looking at her. Dinner be damned.

''No problem,'' he managed to mumble. ''You look…''

For three long beats John wasn't sure how to adequately describe her beauty. And then he realized he was making an utter fool of himself. Whether it was his own rationale that kicked in or the distressed look on her face, he couldn't say for sure. But she looked vastly uncomfortable, stupefying him all over again.

''Great,'' he croaked as the flush of embarrassment climbed up his neck.

She smiled, her lips trembling just the slightest bit. ''Thank you. You look…great…yourself.''

Now he knew exactly how idiotic he'd sounded. ''Shall we?'' He gestured toward the dining room.

She nodded stiffly and preceded him when she ascertained that he was waiting for her to go first. Before he could mull over her awkwardness when it came to formality, her gently swaying hips captured his full attention. That softly rounded derriere moving so alluringly from side to side sent a flood of red-hot desire straight to his loins. He wondered if her slow, almost deliberate steps were a calculated seduction. If so, she had it down to a science.

He blinked then forced one foot in front of the other. God help him. He was doomed and the woman had scarcely spoken to him. How on earth would he ever get to know her better if he couldn't keep his mind off her physical attributes? Off taking her to bed…now?

Dinner conversation consisted of nothing more than silver clinking against china and the sound of wine spilling into crystal. The food smelled heavenly and tasted so good Amy could scarcely think of anything else. Each morsel she lifted to her mouth caused an explosion of the taste buds on her tongue. She'd never, ever had steak like this. The potatoes were sliced, sautéed and spiced in such a way that made them all but melt in her mouth. And the green beans were just shy of crisp with a hint of butter for glazing. The perfect contrast of scents, textures and tastes.

Her second glass of wine had provided a warm fuzzy feeling that accentuated the delectable flavors teasing her mouth. She couldn't recall ever enjoying a meal more.

Then her gaze tangled with her host's and a new kind of warmth surged through her. Watching his lips close around the loaded tines of his fork or nestle around the rim of his wine glass evoked a kind of restlessness deep inside her. She couldn't precisely explain it. Maybe it was the wine exaggerating her perception. But simply watching him eat made her hot. More than that, it made her want to climb across the table and attack him.

Dismayed at her reaction, she fanned a tendril of hair from her face and forced her attention back to her plate. How foolish could she get? Really. She wasn't here to become infatuated with the man. She was here, she reminded herself as she sawed off another sliver of delicious steak, to find out if he was hiding anything.

Like mob-connected activities.

Her brow crinkled as she considered what type of mob activities would take place in Texas. She imagined oil-related, or maybe drugs smuggled in across the southern border. She glanced at John once more and her first gut instinct was that he wouldn't be involved in any such endeavors. But then she remembered the notes attached to his report and she had to look at this objectively. There was the possibility.

This was her chance to find out. To get closer than anyone else at the agency possibly could. If she discovered the truth about John Calhoun, good or bad, she would be a hero. She would either save the Winterbornes a great deal of heartache or she would pave the way for the merger, business as well as personal with no questions outstanding.

An ache echoed through her at that last thought. She shook off the silly sensation. She'd only just met the man for goodness sakes. How could she be feeling anything other than professional curiosity?

Somehow she did.

The sooner she admitted that, the better off she'd be. She had to confess, if only to herself, that the man tripped some sort of trigger for her. She was attracted to him, on a physical level. Big-time attracted. It was not a good thing, that was true, but being aware of it would prove beneficial. And if he, as she suspected, was attracted to her, that could prove beneficial as well.

She could use that attraction to learn what she needed to know. But that just didn't feel right. Their gazes collided again, heat swelled inside her. Oh yeah, it felt right…but it wouldn't *be* right. She had to remember that. Maybe she shouldn't have any more wine while on this assignment.

Amy pushed away her plate and stared at the pristine white linen on the table beneath it. She had never been the underhanded type. What if she wasn't capable of playing the part of spy…of undercover agent…without getting all emotionally involved?

No. She fisted her hand in the linen napkin in her lap. She would not admit defeat this soon or this easily. She could do this. She hardened her jaw and forced her gaze up and forward. If the other women of the Colby Agency could do it, so could she.

All she had to do was focus.

John's gaze met hers and another quake of desire shuddered through her.

God, this was not going to be easy.

"Liam makes the best desserts," he said, his tone sounding almost as tension-filled as she felt.

Liam was the man who'd served their dinner. He was older, sixty maybe, and he had scrutinized her as if he suspected her of being a silverware thief. Could he see through her that easily? Or was it just his way?

"I'm afraid I'm stuffed," Amy insisted, uncertain

she could bear another round of Liam's scrutiny, much less more time alone with Mr. Perfect over there.

"Then how about a walk?" her handsome host offered as he pushed back from the table. "Maybe that'll work up your appetite for coffee and dessert."

She managed a negligible nod as he moved around the table and pulled back her chair.

But it wasn't until he took her hand and led her outside into the moonlight that she really knew she was in serious trouble.

"I'll bet you don't have stars like this in Chicago," he suggested as he peered up at the sky.

Amy started to answer, but the view took away her ability to speak as well as her breath. The black canvas of the night sky spread out endlessly before her. Stars glistened like diamonds splashed across its vast velvety surface.

Oh, yes, he would be right about that. Apparently there were a good many things down here in Texas that she didn't have back home—would never have. Those sexy blue eyes locked with her hungry ones and awareness quivered across her heated skin like the greedy fingers of a skilled lover.

And that was precisely why she had to say goodnight with no possibility of coffee or dessert.

She was far too sure that the dessert would be way more than she was prepared to accept.

Those blue eyes continued to stare directly into hers.

Way, way more.

Chapter Five

Amy lay in bed the next morning, awake well before dawn and listening for the house to grow quiet again.

She'd heard sounds downstairs while the sun still hovered just below the horizon, its fire sending orange tentacles reaching into the gray sky. She'd heard a rusty laugh and determined that the sound belonged to Liam, the man who seemed to look after the house. Amy imagined a maid would show up a couple of times per week. The place was entirely too large for one man, especially an older man, to take care of.

John's answering laugh had drawn her into the hall outside her bedroom. The deep, generous sound of his laughter tugged at some part of her that felt starved for the sound. Reminded her all too much of last night's moonlight walk.

She'd wanted him to kiss her. When she'd insisted on calling it a night she'd seen the want in his eyes as well. He hadn't liked her going in, but, living up to the reputation of a Texas gentleman, he'd relented without argument.

She hugged herself and rubbed at the goose bumps on her arms, rationalizing that an early-morning chill had caused the prickled flesh. Deep down, however, she knew better. Geez, no wonder so many of the Colby agents went out on assignment and ended up married to their principal, whether client or target. Maybe it was the thread of danger surrounding an assignment. After all, if John Calhoun actually did have ties to the mob, uncovering such a connection could be hazardous to her health. So far she'd spent all her time admiring rather than investigating the man.

Slipping back into her room she decided it was time she started doing what she came here to do: investigating. By the time she had showered and pulled on the pale green slacks and striped blouse, silence spread throughout the house.

Tugging on first one sandal then the other, she made her way down the hall, thankful for the nice, flat heels. At the top of the staircase she paused to listen once more. Not a sound. She descended the stairs as quietly as possible considering there was no carpet runner, just bare oak treads. She checked the great room and entry hall, going as far as opening the front door and peeking out into the warm July morning.

Birds chirped in the fresh air and somewhere in the distance she heard what sounded like a horse galloping. She wondered if John had taken an early-morning ride. Maybe he had fences to check or some other cowboy duty.

The kitchen as well as the rest of the downstairs

portion of the house proved to be vacant of human occupation. Her main concern at the moment was where Liam might be. If John was out and about on the ranch, what would his house manager be up to?

A pad on the counter with a well-used pencil lying beside it snagged Amy's attention. Glancing left then right once more, she moved to the counter and peered at the pad. Indentions on the clean page told her that someone had used the pad to make notes. Unsure whether she would learn anything relevant she picked up the pencil and holding it parallel to the pad she rubbed the lead over the blank page. In mere seconds she had covered the page and could read the words formed by the clean indentions: *Supply List.* A list of canned and dried goods followed.

Liam had gone into town for supplies. Amy tore off and wadded the page she'd marked on, quickly disposing of it in the trash receptacle. Since she couldn't be sure how long Liam would be gone it was best to get on with her business.

The home office was down the main corridor beyond the staircase. She retraced her steps, then took a moment to quiet her respiration as she stood in the middle of the spacious office. Natural light flowed in from the large windows that flanked one wall. She listened for several more seconds to make sure no one had come inside while her blood roared in her ears. She had to be calm. This was her first and best shot at proving herself to her boss. She couldn't screw this up by making a mistake or letting her fear get the best of her.

With painstaking slowness, she methodically screened the files in each drawer, starting with the desk. Using up precious time, she opened each folder that wasn't specifically about horses and perused the contents. The oil business she could see being a part of something sinister, but horses? Not likely. He took in the horses, using his vast property for a safe haven of sorts, no money was involved. She'd probably check later just to be sure.

The irony of that fact in contrast to what she suspected of his business dealings wasn't lost on her. Why would a man cold-hearted enough to do business with the mob take in homeless, endangered horses?

Okay, so even criminals could have soft places in their hearts. Any soft spot would definitely have to be in his heart because every other part about him appeared to be as solid as granite. Amy shook off the shivery sensations that accompanied that thought.

Keep your mind on business, girl, she ordered.

She closed the final file cabinet drawer and moved to the computer. She wondered vaguely if others would have started with the computer. With a shrug she set to the task of scanning electronic files.

Having lost all track of time Amy was startled to see that more than an hour had passed by the time she reviewed the final file on John's computer. She'd been in here entirely too long. As quickly as possible she exited the file, her pulse shooting into top speed.

A muffled sound from down the hall paralyzed her.

She strained to hear, her fingers frozen on the keyboard. A chill raced over the perspiration suddenly dampening her skin.

The sound came again.

Closer this time.

''Ms. Winterborne, I presume.''

Amy's head snapped up at the sound of the deep, booming voice. Her gaze locked with a fierce blue one that spoke of decades of hard living and a whole lifetime of cunning. The piercing gaze was set in a face that, though much older, greatly resembled that of her host. Tall and broad-shouldered, he lounged in the doorway, his relaxed posture belying the sharpness in his eyes.

His father.

John Robert Calhoun, III.

J.R.

The jig was up. He'd caught her red-handed and, unlike his son, the buzz of attraction would not turn that suspicion she saw in his eyes to some other less-threatening emotion.

Amy swallowed hard and resisted the urge to jump to her feet. That would only magnify the situation, make her look even guiltier. Instead, she produced a bright smile, one she hoped like hell would at least break the ice glazing the old coot's eyes.

''Good morning. You must be John's father.''

He pushed off from the door frame and ambled across the room. ''That's me.'' He lifted his Stetson and smoothed one broad hand over his gray-blond hair. "John put you to work for him?" he asked casually with a discreet nod toward the computer.

She made a sound, half laugh, half sigh. "Oh, no." She glanced at the computer and shook her head. "I was just trying to figure out if I could check my e-mail from here." She rolled her eyes and made a self-deprecating sound. "I swear I can't go anywhere overnight without worrying that I might miss something."

J.R. nodded. "I know what you mean. I like to stay on top of things myself."

Renewed fear inched up her spine. He was playing it loosely but she could read the signs. She'd studied body language and recognized his continued suspicion from the way he didn't look directly at her when he spoke now and the hands that eventually parked on his hips. He thought she was lying through her teeth.

"Do you mind?" she prodded. "I'd just sat down when you came in."

That wise gaze narrowed. "Make yourself at home, little lady. I'm going in here to find out what Liam's planning for brunch."

She forced another smile. "Give me a moment and I'll go with you," she said, to his complete surprise. The look now claiming his face told her that he hadn't expected that. Chalk one up for her.

While he waited patiently, discreetly glancing her way from time to time, she quickly found the Internet access and went to the home page of her personal server and opened her Web mail.

She giggled and shook her head. "Can you believe it? My friend Jenny dumped her boyfriend and got a dog." Logging out she looked up at J. R. Calhoun. "I predict that will never last."

He chuckled as she skirted the desk. "A good dog is a fine thing," he offered sagely. "But it won't keep you warm at night like the love of a good man will."

Their gazes locked once more and she read the uncertainty in his. J.R. might be all for his son's marriage to a stranger for the good of the company, but he still wanted only the best for his one and only son. All she had to do was look into those piercing blue depths to know that. The intensity there completely unnerved her.

"I agree," she said when she found her voice once more. "What good is anything else if you're not happy?"

Amy wasn't sure what had made her say that last part. But it was true. J.R. had looked away when she said it. Looked away and hurriedly led her to the kitchen where Liam was unloading his newly purchased supplies.

Accepting a cup of coffee, Amy scooted onto a stool by the kitchen's center island and watched the two men scurry about. Liam knew right where he wanted everything and J.R. only seemed to get in the way, but neither would give an inch. J.R. insisted on helping and Liam fought him every step of the way. Finally the two converged on preparing Saturday brunch.

"We have brunch together every Sunday," J.R. explained, glancing over his shoulder from his position at the extra-wide commercial stove top. "But since you're here I thought I'd drop by today as well."

"Advance warning wouldn't kill you," Liam grumbled. He apparently didn't like disruptions in his usual routine.

"What?" J.R. demanded good-naturedly. "And take all the fun out of listening to you complain? No way."

Amy had offered to help twice but the men insisted she keep her seat. She was a guest.

"Has this always been the family home?" she asked when the sparring lulled.

J.R. nodded. "John's mother designed the house. She was an architect and decorator. Damn good at it, too."

That was easy to see. The floor plan of the house was flawless. A smooth flow from room to room. "The decor is perfect for the house," she noted aloud. "Homey with just a hint of formality. I like it."

"Yeah," J.R. said proudly. "I reckon John inherited her ability to pull together a room."

Amy frowned. "He did the decorating?"

"My Stella passed away a long time ago, Miss Regina, it was time the place was updated." He looked around him, as if admiring all over again his son's work. "His mother would be proud of what he's done. God knows I never changed anything while I was here."

"You don't live here anymore?" Okay, it was a

personal question she knew, but she just had to have the answer. The place was enormous. There was definitely room for one more. Though she was pretty sure no one else had come in last night. She'd lain there for hours unable to sleep, wondering about John Calhoun. And then she'd gone to sleep and dreamed about him. She banished the memory, determined not to fall into that trap again. She had to keep her head on straight today.

Another of those throaty chuckles reverberated from J.R. "Well, I decided to move out a while back. John needed his space and I needed mine," he said in answer to her question.

Liam made a harrumphing sound. "More like you needed a bachelor lair." He tossed a knowing look at Amy. "The man don't go a single night 'cept Fridays and Sundays without a supper date."

J.R. shrugged sheepishly. "A man's gotta eat, don't he?"

"You could eat at a restaurant," Liam shot back.

Amy couldn't help but laugh. The two had obviously been at this a lifetime. Her mother and father were like that. Always teasing each other, pretending to argue, when anyone who knew them recognized it for what it was—true love.

Oh, if only she could find a life partner like that.

"Well, I see you've met Dad."

She swiveled abruptly, almost falling off the stool, at the sound of John's voice in the doorway. Instantly a smile tipped her lips upward.

"I did, indeed," she mused.

She didn't have to explain, from the expression on his face he fully understood and then he smiled at her. She melted just a little.

"I thought for a minute it was Sunday," he said to his father.

J.R. offered another of those nonchalant shrugs. "I didn't have anything special to do today. Thought I'd come over and make Miss Regina's acquaintance," he retorted. "Besides, I didn't know I needed an invitation."

"You don't." John set his hat aside and settled on a stool next to Amy. "She prefers being called Gina, by the way."

J.R. looked from his son to Amy. "Why didn't you say something?"

"It's okay, really," she hastened to assure him. She definitely hadn't wanted to say anything to the man. It wasn't even her name anyway. She bounced a nervous glance between the two. Liam kept his attention on the sizzling bacon and sausage. Amy's stomach rumbled in spite of her rising tension.

"Flat cakes or waffles?" J.R. wanted to know, changing the subject, to her immense relief.

"Either one would be great."

"Do you ride?" This question came from the man at her side.

"Ride?" She stared up at John, scared to death that he meant horses. Not that she had anything against the beautiful animals, but she'd never climbed on one and didn't have any intention of doing so. Images of rearing, bucking horses immediately flashed through her mind.

"Don't be afraid," he said, reading her mind and clearly finding her anxiety amusing. "I'll teach you everything you need to know."

And just like that the decision was made. She would ride a raging bull if it meant John Calhoun was going to teach her how.

JOHN SADDLED UP the old bay mare since she was the gentlest in the stable. She wouldn't give Gina any trouble. His lips stretched into a little smile as he considered his father's showing up the way he had this morning. The old man hadn't been able to wait to get a look at his prospective daughter-in-law. He'd given John the nod of approval…a nod punctuated by a broad grin. J.R. Calhoun liked her.

Speaking of his bridal candidate, John noted that as he tightened the cinch and went through the final checks of her riding gear, Gina nervously paced the barn behind him.

"I'm really not sure this is a good idea," she said eventually, offering a magnanimous wave of her arms. "I'm certain I'll be terrible at it and—"

"You'll be fine. Trust me." He offered her another of those wide, enchanting smiles, but it didn't seem to help. Unable to resist, he took another moment to admire her. The slacks and blouse were quite flattering. The colors looked good on her, but it was the fit that twisted his insides into knots of relentless desire. The little sandals weren't exactly riding shoes, but they'd have to do. He would keep an eye on her footing as she mounted and dismounted. His gaze moved hungrily back up to her face where she chewed nervously on her lower lip. He liked that little habit, it made him want to use his tongue, his lips to soothe the flesh she tortured.

Who would have thought that a business merger would send him exactly what he would have ordered were he to mail-order a bride?

Her long hair was pulled back into a ponytail today, giving him full visual access to the soft lines of her cheek, the arrogant little tilt of her chin and the small but pert profile of her nose. God, she was pretty. He hadn't seen the first indication of anything wicked about her. Was she really all that he'd read she was? Selfish, self-indulgent and with a sexual appetite that didn't appear quenchable? Somehow that Regina Winterborne just didn't jibe with the one standing before him. There had to be a mistake.

Either that or he was the biggest fool in Texas.

"Come on over here and let me give you a lift," he urged. "You'll never forgive yourself if you don't give horseback riding a try."

She still looked hesitant but curiosity had peeked through the worry lines. He could almost see her weighing the concept in her mind, considering the pros and cons. How could she be the impetuous girl who had been described to him?

"Okay," she said on a mighty breath. "If you're sure I'm not going to do myself bodily injury."

He laughed. "I can promise you that you're completely safe on old Bessy here. She doesn't even bother swishing her tail at flies anymore."

Darting a skeptical look at the horse's tail, Gina moved cautiously toward him. "All I have to do is pull back on the reins and she'll stop, right?"

Those wide brown eyes peered up at him, a world of fear laced with anticipation shimmering there. "Just don't pull too hard."

Her breath caught. "What's too hard?"

"Come on, honey, you'll be fine."

Their eyes met and a blast of heat exploded between them. He hadn't meant to call her honey, but the reaction was definitely worth it. Mercy, there was some serious chemistry going on here.

She reached for the saddle horn and he reached for her waist. She froze, her backside now resting intimately against his front. Though he couldn't say for sure, he felt reasonably positive that neither of them breathed for one endless moment. The subtle aroma of roses filled his nostrils as he took a necessary breath and his eyes closed while his senses reveled in the scent and feel of her.

Forcing his eyes open and his mind on the task at hand, his entire body tightened with need as his lips brushed the soft skin of her cheek when he murmured, "I'll give you a lift, all you have to do is swing your right leg over."

She nodded, the movement scarcely perceptible.

Not wanting to release her and end the moment, he gritted his teeth and did just what he'd said he would. She settled into the saddle and smiled tremulously down at him.

His hands fisted at his sides, his fingers already missing the feel of her sleek body. "You look good in a saddle," he said softly, his mind instantly conjuring images of her sitting astride him like that...of him nestled deep between her thighs.

AMY SAT perfectly still until he snapped out of the coma he'd appeared to have fallen into and mounted his horse. She wasn't sure she wanted to analyze what she thought she saw in his eyes. Not good for keeping her head on straight, she decided as he moved up beside her. The last smile she'd managed to give him was still frozen on her face. She didn't dare move a muscle for fear the animal would bolt. Unblinking, she mentally uttered a desperate prayer that God would get her through this day. This day? She hoped He could get her through the weekend.

She'd searched the files in John's office, paper as well as electronic, had surveyed his private e-mails. Unless the man was hiding something at his business office, he was squeaky clean. There had to be some sort of mistake. But the Colby Agency didn't make mistakes.

John made a clicking sound with his tongue and his horse moved forward, Bessy did the same. All thoughts of mob connections and investigations flew right out of her head. The only thing on Amy's mind at that moment was clinging to the saddle. She locked her thighs in place and grabbed for the saddle horn. If this horse bucked, she planned to stay in place as if she'd been Velcroed there.

They rode for what felt like hours. John spoke from time to time, pointing out some landmark. Amy had relaxed a bit. Her thighs quivered from the tension. She'd discovered thankfully that her horse appeared happy moving along at a nice slow pace. She hadn't bucked or reared. And, truth be told, Amy was beginning to enjoy the ride.

The scenery was amazing. Lush green pastures, a clump of trees here and there. But the real stunner came when they reached the river. The view took her breath away.

The water flowed slowly, trickling over the occasional rock jutting above its surface. From where she sat it looked crystal-clear. She was suddenly desperately thirsty.

"Let me help you down."

John was standing right beside her and she hadn't even realized he'd dismounted.

Allowing him to grasp her waist once more as she swung her leg over the horse's rear, she lost her breath all over again. The moment his fingers closed around her something warm and exciting licked through her, like flames on a cold winter's night. He held on a second or two longer than necessary once she was safely on the ground.

"This is my favorite place," he said, those startling blue eyes holding hers when she turned to face him.

"I can see why." Actually the only thing she saw at the moment was him. She just couldn't stop staring up at him. But she'd gotten a good look at the view while atop the horse. "It's beautiful."

He was the first to avert his gaze. "My mother and I used to picnic here when I was just a boy."

She could hear how much he'd loved his mother. "What about your father?" The question was out of her mouth before she could stop it. She seemed to always go for the most personal ones first.

His gaze grew distant and he considered her question for a time before he answered. "Times were tough for a few years during my childhood and Dad was away a lot." He looked down at her, his gaze slowly coming back into focus. "But he made up for it later."

Somehow that relieved her. Amy didn't want to hear anything bad about the man she'd met that morning. She wanted him to be the loving father—and husband—he appeared to be when he spoke of his family. Not to mention the master chef. She wasn't sure who was the best, J.R. or Liam. The two men had a regular contest going over who could make the best flat cakes. It would have been such a shame for any of that to be a lie.

Like you, a little voice taunted.

Amy turned away from John to stride determinedly toward the water's edge. As much as she couldn't bear to look into his eyes anymore, the first step she took almost stopped her dead in her tracks. She was stiff from riding. Her butt actually felt numb, as did her thighs from clutching at the saddle for so long before she relaxed. She had an almost overwhelming urge to reach back and pluck at the thong that had crawled well beyond where it was meant to be. It would definitely take a long hot soak in the tub to undo this kind of damage.

"Tell me about your childhood," he said softly as he came up beside her after having seen to the horses.

Panic burgeoned in her throat. What did she do now? She knew nothing about Regina Winterborne's childhood. But she had to think of something otherwise he'd become suspicious.

"I don't want to talk about me right now," she said, adopting a smile and fluttering her eyes flirtatiously at him. "I want to hear more about you."

"Tell you what," he countered, something primal flaring to life in those deep baby blues. The primitive invitation jerked on some thread connected to her feminine core that seemed to be coiling more tightly inside her with each passing second in his presence. "How about we have a little afternoon snack and we'll play truth or dare. You up for it?"

Renewed panic broadsided her. "Are we going back already?" she asked, her voice undeniably strangled.

He nodded toward the scattering of trees a few yards

away. "Liam dropped off a snack for us. Riding the range can build up an appetite."

She only nodded, too dumbfounded or worried—no, too scared—to speak. It wasn't until John moved toward the trees that she allowed herself to look. Sure enough, beneath one big old oak tree was a blanket and a picnic basket. Liam had clearly taken a short cut since she hadn't seen him and he appeared to be long gone.

"We took the long way around," John said, confirming her conclusion, as he waited for her to join him. "The scenic route so to speak."

She managed another jerky nod.

"Relax, Gina." He reached for her hand and gave it a squeeze, sending another round of fiery sensations through her. "I was only kidding about the truth or dare. Let's just enjoy the day."

She sat down on the blanket, mostly because her knees had given way with relief.

Liam had outdone himself. Wine, cheese and crackers, fruit. He'd even packed the stemmed crystal. She couldn't help but shake her head. Crystal wasn't exactly what she'd expected on a Texas picnic.

"I think Liam and my dad are working overtime to make us comfortable."

Amy smiled, the first real one since they started out on this journey. "I think you're right."

"There are things we need to talk about, Gina," he said on a more serious note. "Important things. I don't want us to pretend our way through this. It's too important.'' He settled an urgent gaze on hers. ''The truth is all that matters.''

Amy felt her heart drop into the vicinity of her stomach. The truth was the last thing she could talk about.

Chapter Six

By the time they arrived back at the ranch house later that afternoon Amy was sure she would never walk again. Her thighs and buttocks were so stiff, and soreness was already setting in, that she was sure she must have permanent damage. John suggested a hot soak in the tub and apologized again for taking her on such a long tour of his property. He should have known it would be too much for her, he had offered with sincere regret.

She'd smiled and pretended it was nothing, just a touch of stiffness.

Yeah, right.

She groaned as she shifted in the tub, the deep, hot water sloshing around her. If she never rode a horse again it would be too soon. How did these cowboys and cowgirls do it? Being able to sit through dinner tonight might just be physically impossible.

The sound of John's husky laughter echoed in her mind, reminding her of the time they'd spent together under that big old oak tree. She relaxed more deeply into the welcoming depths of the heat surrounding her and replayed their time together on her first romantic picnic.

John Calhoun, IV, was not only a devastatingly handsome man, he was kind, with a sparkling sense of humor. Amy smiled. She had never met a man like him. His wealth had not gone to his head, far from it. He appeared to use his vast financial means for good. Of course he took care of himself and those he considered family, they all drove the latest and most coveted vehicles on the local market. The family home was large and quite grand. His wardrobe, at least what she'd seen thus far, was impeccable and on the expensive side. But none of it made him act in a superior manner. Or if it did, he darn sure hid it well.

No. Amy was certain the man did not possess a single condescending bone. His father appeared to be the one who worried about the money. She remembered something being said about hard times when John had been a child. Probably his father recalled all too well those hard times and focused a bit more on financial security. Amy recognized that same trait in her own parents. Anyone who had gone without didn't soon forget how it felt.

She grew very still, focusing inward for a time before she allowed the rest of the conversation beneath that big tree to filter through her mind.

John wanted a real wife, not a mere partner on paper. He made very clear that his expectations were that the woman he married would share his life and his bed, that they would have children. He'd seemed almost frantic to get that point across to her, as if he feared she might not get it or fully understand it to the extent he meant.

Instantly the image of the real Regina Winterborne unfurled in her mind. Oh God. She was the reason why. Everyone at the agency knew about Regina's exploits. There was something in the society pages about her at least twice a month. The woman went through more boyfriends in a year than most women did in a lifetime. She was reported to be snobbish and, according to Mildred at the office, she was quite selfish and hateful. As much as she hated to admit it, Amy could see that. Only a few minutes in the woman's presence and her obnoxiousness was more than apparent. John or his father had likely done a little investigating of their own and knew of her reputation. No wonder Liam had eyed her so skeptically. He probably thought she was some big-city harlot.

The idea that John might be saddled with that woman for the rest of his life made Amy want to scream at the injustice of it. There had to be a way to warn him…to stop it.

If she found anything negative about him…that could break the deal. She doubted Edgar Winterborne would want to begin a partnership with anyone who had less than a stellar business reputation. Certainly he wouldn't want to thrust his daughter into a life of crime. Mr. Winterborne appeared to be a good deal more scrupulous than his daughter. Maybe that was the key.

But then she'd been all through John's home office and hadn't found a thing.

What if there was nothing to find?

Determined to check one last place at the house, Amy climbed out of the tub and grabbed a large, fluffy towel. Maybe John Calhoun kept his secrets in his private room, his bedroom. She shivered, chalked it up to the cool climate-controlled air in the room, and hurriedly dried her skin and then her long hair. She had at least to check it out. Any good agent would. Drumming up the opportunity to take a look at his business office would be a good deal more complicated.

As quickly as she could, she shimmied into the little black dress, since John had mentioned they would be going out for dinner, then applied a little blush and eye shadow. When she'd arranged her still slightly damp hair into an upswept fashion she stood back and studied her reflection.

Not bad. One thing she could give Regina Winterborne, she had great taste in clothes. Even if the shoes were murder on Amy's insteps.

She listened at the door of her room for several seconds and heard nothing but silence. Liam had the evening off and John was probably still outside. He'd had chores to see to, he'd said. Tamping down the little stir of desire at recalling the way he'd looked at her when they parted ways, she sneaked into the hall and headed in the direction of his room. She'd passed the room once before and noticed the door open. Judging by the jeans on the floor and the shirt thrown across the foot of the bed she'd been relatively certain it was John's.

She glanced covertly left and right one last time before stepping into his private sanctuary.

And it was definitely his room.

One whiff of the aftershave lingering in the air and her body started to throb with need. She closed her eyes and inhaled deeply. The man smelled like heaven on earth. Good enough to eat. She licked her lips. Heat slowly swirled beneath her belly button, spreading outward, making her too warm in the skimpy black dress.

Her eyes snapped open and she mentally scolded herself for the luxury. She had a job to do. Quickly, before she lapsed into another lust-induced trance, she methodically moved about his room, scouring every square inch of his personal space. Quietly, ever so quietly, she checked each drawer, not making so much as a sound. By the time she'd gone through the massive dresser and the highboy armoire, she was quite proud of her stealth.

The framed photographs on his bedside table momentarily captured her attention. John and his father. A much younger John, a teenager, with both his mother and father. Though he had his father's build and eyes, John Calhoun had definitely gotten his amazing good looks from his beautiful mother. She was cover-girl gorgeous.

In the photograph, J.R. was looking at his lovely

wife. The framed moment in time had captured on his face the look of pure love. Amy's heart squeezed. It must have been so hard for him to lose her when they'd had so much life ahead of them. She realized then why J.R. had dinner with a different lady friend every night. He was fighting the loneliness in the only way he knew how. It must have eaten away at him before he broke down and distracted himself.

That was what his son wanted, Amy suddenly knew as well as she knew her own name. That's what this afternoon's little talk had been about. He wanted what his mother and father had shared. He wanted a woman to look at him that way...to cherish him as his mother had cherished his father. He wanted utter trust, a complete bond.

Dear God, he was never in a million years going to get that from Regina Winterborne.

Sympathy and something far too close to jealousy washed over Amy. Their marriage would be a travesty. It would ruin both their lives and their children would pay the heavy price. John's suffering would be immeasurable.

Shaking her head, Amy forced her attention back to business. The bedside table yielded nothing.

She was kidding herself here. She wasn't going to find anything on John Calhoun or his father. They were clean. Good people. Nothing more or less.

There had to be a mistake. Apparently even a Colby agent could make a mistake.

Just then her gaze drifted to the one place she'd carefully kept it steered clear of.

The bed.

John's bed.

It was massive, four-poster like the one in her room. But the bedcovers had a more masculine flair about them. Tans and browns, moss green. The room matched the earthiness of the man. His Stetson lay in the middle of the bed and she suddenly found herself reaching for it. She held it close and breathed deeply of his scent. A hint of the herbal shampoo he used and the slightest essence of good clean sweat.

Her heart began to race and Amy had to close her eyes and struggle to slow its frantic pace. She slowly lowered the hat back to the bed covers and told herself it was time to get out of here before she was caught.

Somehow she had to figure out a way to save John from the fate that lay in store for him.

JOHN HAD WORKED himself up a healthy sweat. The bandana tied around his forehead kept it from running down into his eyes. He smoothed a hand over his bare chest to swipe away the perspiration beading there. He'd had to do something to get his mind off Gina and all the things he'd like to do with her...to her.

Like make long, slow love.

They'd barely met twenty-four hours ago and already he was certain she was the one for him.

She didn't like to talk about herself, he'd had to prod every answer out of her and even those were vague. She adored her father and to his surprise loved the same kind of movies he did—thrillers. He loved the chase…the building suspense whether slow mounting or fast-paced. His mother had loved that kind as well, especially the ones where the damsel in distress was rescued by the dashing hero. God, he'd loved those Friday nights at the movies with his mom. He still missed her.

A smile tugged as his mouth as he thought of the way his mother would tell his dad all about the movie. John often wondered if his dad had really loved poker night so much or if he just preferred hearing the story told by the woman he loved. Maybe that's why John suffered such agony over this decision yawning before him. He'd wanted what he knew his mother and father had shared. He'd been very nearly certain he wasn't going to find it in this lifetime. Certainly not as part of a business merger. And lo and behold, the gods had truly shone on him after all. He could definitely fall in love with Gina. She was sweet and kind, seriously easy on the eyes and he'd never met a woman who radiated more innocence.

He'd dated more than his fair share and the debutantes with whom he'd waltzed away a night or two had been experienced women who'd known what they wanted and had made no qualms about going after it. He sensed none of that in Gina. She appeared to have no hidden agenda. He liked that about her. Really liked it.

Damn if he could figure out what her father had

meant by warning him that she was impetuous and petulant. Hell, from all he'd seen, she reasoned quite thoroughly before making a move or answering a question.

Even the report Nate had gotten from his private investigator had been utterly negative. It had touted her numerous affairs and wild behavior. Where was that woman? Because the one he'd spent the last twenty-four hours with was not that person.

Unless she'd been tutored.

He halted, midreach, his hands halfway to their destination—the next bag of oats. Straightening up the barn wasn't usually his job, but he'd felt compelled to occupy himself with physical labor so he'd given his ranch hands the rest of the day off and had thrown himself into completing the last of the necessary chores. Otherwise he might just explode with sexual frustration.

What if Edgar Winterborne had instructed his daughter on how she was to behave? He, of all people, was well aware of what John expected. And he definitely wouldn't want his daughter to screw this up. It was in his best interest as well as her own from a financial perspective. On a more personal note he could see the old man wanting his daughter to be settled with the kind of man who would take good care of her. Especially if she was as wild as he claimed.

This whole weekend could be nothing but a show. A way to prove to John that she was the right woman for him. To inspire trust. To put the final touches on the deal of a lifetime.

John's lifetime.

Nausea roiled in his gut. Could he be that blind? Could the woman he'd spent this seemingly special time with really be that good an actress?

His fingers clenched into fists and his jaw hardened at the idea. Just as suddenly another part of him refuted that conclusion. No way could anyone fake that kind of sincerity. She was for real. He was sure of it.

He refused to believe the sweetness of her smile and the vulnerability he saw in her eyes was all an act.

Maybe he was a fool, but he'd bet everything on his instincts.

This woman was the one for him.

John glanced at his watch and swore. He was late. He'd have to rush through a shower in order to be ready on time.

He had big plans for tonight. He wanted to show Gina off around town and for her to get an idea of what life here was like. His hometown was nothing like Chicago. She needed to be aware of that. Somehow he felt sure that wasn't going to be an issue.

The lady would fit in anywhere.

The only question that remained as far as he was concerned was whether or not she was as convinced that they could have a future together as he was.

Unless something drastic happened, his mind was made up.

RUNAWAY BAY was nothing at all like Chicago but it was a lovely town. It looked country, the perfect setting for boots and Stetsons and pickup trucks, but it was citified enough to fulfill most all one's shopping needs and just about anything else she could think of.

Amy had never loved city life, not completely anyway. Her parents had raised her in a small farming community outside Chicago, a place not unlike this one, only without the hats and boots and with slightly fewer trucks. She'd walked to school every day, had joined her friends at the skating rink on Saturday afternoons. This was that kind of town. And she liked it already.

"This reminds me of—" Amy stopped midsentence. She'd almost said *home.* "Of…of a little place outside Chicago where a friend of mine lived when we were growing up. I always loved spending the night with her. We'd walk to the skating rink." She noticed a Dairy Dip and smiled. "There was a place just like that." She pointed to the little oldfashioned place. "We always got an ice-cream cone on our way home after skating."

John, sans his Stetson, smiled at her. "I've been known to hang out there myself." He chuckled. "A decade or so ago."

They shared a laugh together and it felt good.

Too good.

How was she ever going to tell him the truth? He was going to be angry and hurt. She would likely lose her job. As much as she wanted to be a Colby agent, losing that opportunity felt like nothing compared to the other thing she was going to lose. There would be absolutely no way she could make this right with John. Any possible future together was out of the question.

Hurt arced in her chest. Who was she kidding? They'd never had a chance. She wouldn't even be here with him if he didn't think she was some rich oil heiress from the Windy City. He likely wouldn't even have taken a second look at her. He could have his choice of women. Of that she was sure. There was no telling how many had already tried to win his affections—and ultimately—his money.

Amy studied his profile. It had to be hard, dealing with that whole concept. How would he know when a woman cared about him rather than his money?

Sincerity could be faked. To an extent anyway. She closed her eyes and chewed her lower lip to stem the rush of tears. But none of that mattered now. He was taken. The deal had been made, only the technicalities remained. He would be utterly miserable with Regina Winterborne. Amy knew that for a certainty. The selfish snob she had met didn't deserve a man like John Calhoun.

"Here we are," he announced as he braked to make a left turn.

Amy opened her eyes and blinked back the moisture. Runaway Bay Country Club. Well, she'd never been to a country club before. She doubted she would fit in, but, she suddenly decided right then and there, she would give it her best shot. This would be her last night as Miss Regina Winterborne. Tomorrow she would tell John the truth. She couldn't let this go any further. Whatever trouble awaited her when Victoria discovered her ruse, this wasn't fair to John. That was the worst part. She'd lied to him, allowed him to believe in that lie. Tomorrow she'd come clean, face the consequences.

But tonight she intended to have her night at the ball. To play Cinderella just this once. To live the fantasy. What could it hurt? The damage was done. It wasn't like telling him now would make any real difference versus telling him tomorrow.

The lights from the country club's grand entrance glowed, cutting a path across the dark parking area. The moon, masked by clouds, provided little in the way of assistance. The breeze wasn't exactly cool but it was nice all the same. Amy was pretty sure that had it been an arctic blast she'd still have been warm as long as she walked next to John. Just looking at him made her blood sizzle in her veins, made her think wicked thoughts. The kind that would get her in more trouble than she was already in. Not a good thing.

"Do you come here often?" she heard herself ask, suddenly needing to know if she would meet women here he'd dated or who chased after him still. Would she be the envy of a number of those present? She couldn't imagine any female still breathing wouldn't feel just a tad envious that he didn't belong to them. She almost shook her head at her foolishness. Where did she get off asking such a personal question? She'd done it all day.

"Occasionally. There's a dance every Saturday night during the summer months. I've been known to show up every couple of weeks."

It dawned on her then that he would expect her to ask just such a question. A prospective wife would, after all, want to know all about the man she planned to wed.

He reached for her arm and wrapped it around his, urging her closer. "But this time will be special."

For just one moment their eyes met beneath the glimmer of the entrance lights and she saw the longing in his…the same longing she felt. This attraction had evolved into something stronger, deeper maybe. Definitely not a good thing.

John made the rounds, introducing the woman at his side to his friends and those he associated with on a professional level. Young and old, most of the gentlemen in the area brought their wives to the club at least once a month. It was a kind of tradition, an opportunity to show off, maybe do a little good-natured bragging. The wives showed off their latest jewels and designer dresses while the husbands bragged about their latest business conquests. Then there was the singles set, who did pretty much the same thing only with the additional element of attempting to show up with the most sought-after date.

That was one part about bachelorhood that John definitely would not miss. Though he couldn't say that he hadn't enjoyed the company of numerous lovely ladies, the bigger part of him wanted a family, longed for stability.

He just hadn't expected to get it in quite this manner. He watched Gina as she chatted with the wives of two of his friends. He'd thought she looked amazing in that emerald dress last night, but it didn't hold a candle to the little black one she wore tonight. He'd almost dragged her up to his room and locked the door the moment he laid eyes on her. The very idea that other men would look at her, would see—he drew in a deep breath and let it out slowly—all that beauty cinched in black silk was just about more than he could bear.

But he had to do this right.

He definitely hadn't expected to feel any of this. Not this soon anyway. Hadn't expected ever to be happy with an arranged marriage. But now that he'd met her, had gotten to know her just a little, everything was different. John had never been one to believe in love at first sight, though his mother had insisted that she and his father had fallen in love in that very manner. Still, he'd always harbored serious doubts about the whole notion. Now he knew what his mother had been talking about.

The way his attraction had grown and evolved since first laying eyes on Gina scarcely more than twenty-four hours ago certainly qualified as love at first sight.

He'd always been of the mind that anything too good to be true probably was, but not Gina. She was the one for him. They could make this work, he felt certain.

The band struck up a slow song and John smiled. It was time he found out whether or not his lady could dance. He made his way through the milling group and sidled up next to her, whispering for her ears only. "How about a dance, pretty lady?"

She looked up at him and his heart did one hell of a somersault. "Why, I thought you'd never ask, cowboy."

The moment he had her in his arms all else ceased to exist. The people, the place, even the music. There was only the woman in his arms and that moment. She followed his lead as gracefully as he'd known she would, almost floating across the floor as they two-stepped to the sensual rise and fall of the music's tempo. Those dark-brown eyes tugged at him, made him want to hold her closer, made him want to kiss her.

But not here…he wanted their first kiss to be special.

Later, when he had her back home that moment would come and he would do all within his power to make it a kiss she would never forget.

AFTER PARKING, John opened the passenger-side door, lifted Amy from the seat and lowered her until her feet touched the ground once more. Still she felt as if she were floating.

As they moved toward the silent house she smiled,

thinking of all the dances they'd shared. Of how wonderful it had felt to be held in his strong arms…of how hot and bothered she'd grown right there in the middle of all those people.

It wasn't until the night was over and they'd floated from the dance floor that she realized how focused they had been on one another the whole evening. They'd scarcely spoken a word to anyone after the initial introductions. It hadn't mattered if the band played a slow song or a fast, funky beat, they had been lost to their own little world, their own tempo.

But now it was over.

Once inside the entry hall, Amy waited for him to lock up before she said good-night. This was it, time for the fantasy to fade back into reality. She would sleep, dream of being in John's arms and then in the morning she would tell him the truth and head for the airport.

He would hate her. She'd be unemployed. But, incredibly, it was almost worth it.

How many times in one's life did one have the opportunity to know this kind of fantasy? Rarely, if ever. This was her moment. She'd cherish it forever. The bottom line professionally speaking was that she was only an assistant. She'd probably never have gotten promoted to an agent anyway. At least she'd got one of her two dreams—the fantasy lover, if only for one weekend.

"Thank you for a wonderful time, John," she said

when he turned to face her. She still sounded a little breathless, but who wouldn't?

Those hypnotic blue eyes peered deeply into hers. "It's not over yet."

"It's late and—"

And then he kissed her.

The moment their lips touched, light and sensation burst between them, around them, inside them. Shattering like the thinnest, most delicate of glass... sending shard after shard of desire, need, want spraying over them.

Amy knew she shouldn't allow this, told herself to pull away. But she simply couldn't manage the necessary action.

His arms went around her, drawing her nearer as his mouth leveled more fully onto hers. The tingle started in her toes and rushed all the way up to her scalp, leaving a path of heat that threatened to incinerate her from the inside out. Never had she been kissed like this...he tugged on her bottom lip with his teeth, teased her greedy mouth with his tongue, and then ravished her to the point of insanity. She clung to his shoulders, her legs having gone limp beneath her from the boiling of her blood. Every nerve in her body was throbbing. Every fiber of her being felt on fire. The very core of her being verged on explosion.

His hands slid down over her bottom, cupped her intimately, and then he did this little move that tipped her completely over the edge. He rocked her pelvis against his and she came...in one violent rush she reached the absolute pinnacle standing right there in the entry hall with both of them fully clothed.

She drew back, her breath catching hard. His gaze locked with hers, took a moment to focus before she read the same shock she felt.

"Good night," she squeaked before bolting for the staircase.

Whether too confused or too startled to react she couldn't say, she was just damn glad he didn't follow her.

She'd fallen to pieces in his arms with no more prodding than a kiss. She cringed as she flew into her room and slammed the door behind her. How pathetic was that? Granted, it was one hell of a kiss…but just a kiss. Tell that to her body, she mused, sinking to the floor as the final waves of completion washed through her.

Moments later when she'd caught her breath and her face had ceased to burn with humiliation, she told herself that it was a good thing. She would never get to sleep with him, much less marry him, but at least she had the best orgasm of her life to remember him by.

That was something.

Chapter Seven

Nate Beckman waited impatiently as the telephone rang for the fifth time. It was early on a Sunday morning, surely Mr. Winterborne hadn't left for morning services already. He picked up his cup and sipped his coffee, enjoying the warm chicory taste.

Just then the ringing stopped and a rushed voice said, "Winterborne."

"Good morning, Edgar. Nate Beckman here." Nate leaned forward in his leather executive chair and scanned the photos scattered across his desk. A satisfied smile slid across his freshly shaven face. Oh, things were working out just fine. Just fine indeed.

"Beckman, is there something wrong, man?"

Ever the loving father, Nate mused. His daughter was always his highest priority. The man definitely needed a partner before he ran his company into the ground. The very idea that he would allow his daughter to run through the major portion of his ready cash flow. What a waste. Nate frowned. He'd been more than a little surprised by the young woman. He hadn't expected such a well-behaved, seemingly *nice* girl. He'd expected a wildcat. One who would instantly send John running for the hills.

He looked at the pictures once more, especially those taken by the river. That definitely had not happened. Everything was falling into place.

"No, no, Edgar, all is well. That's why I'm calling."

"I'll be ready for the one o'clock flight. Has there been a change in the itinerary?" Edgar cleared his throat. "I suppose there's no chance I could speak with my daughter this morning."

Now came the touchy part. "Actually, Edgar, I was hoping to convince you to delay your arrival until tomorrow."

"What?" A rattling sound echoed across the line as if he were changing positions or had lunged to his feet. "Why would I want to wait? My daughter is expecting me this afternoon. I don't see—"

"Let me explain," Nate interrupted smoothly, before the man worked himself into a complete frenzy. "Things are actually going far better than we could have anticipated. You should see them together. It's amazing. I've never seen two more starry-eyed lovers."

"Really?" Surprise was cram-packed behind that one word.

"It's unbelievable. They hit it off almost immediately and yesterday evolved into a smashing success. That's why I'm calling. I've spoken to J.R. and he agrees. We'd like to give them another twenty-four hours alone. We feel it's imperative that this budding relationship set awhile longer before reality intrudes. Any external presence, you or J.R., might hinder that steady progression. J.R. has agreed to stay clear for the day, if you'll agree to the same."

Silence radiated on the other end of the line for several seconds that quickly turned to a full tension-filled minute. Nate had just about decided that the man wasn't going to go along with the idea when he finally spoke.

"You're right. We should let this go where it will without interference. I want this to work. I want my daughter to be safe and happy."

Nate picked up one picture in particular that showed John and Gina picnicking by the water's edge. The smile on the young woman's face glowed with happiness. "I don't think you have a thing to worry about, Edgar. This is definitely going the way we'd hoped. Hell, better than we'd hoped. I'd reached the conclusion that the two merely tolerating each other would be acceptable."

Edgar sighed. "Yes, that's all I'd hoped for as well. So you say they've truly hit it off?"

"Absolutely. I can hear the wedding bells already."

"All right then," Edgar said in finality. "Send your plane for me tomorrow morning around nine your time. I'd like to be at the ranch in time for an afternoon lunch."

"Done."

Nate ended the call and leaned back in triumph. He'd known he could make this happen. When he'd first approached J.R. with the idea the man had thought he'd lost his mind. Winterborne had merely laughed at the prospect. He, apparently, knew his daughter too well. Or thought he did. But Nate knew John, he would sacrifice his own comfort and happiness for his father, for the good of the company in a heartbeat. On the other hand, Regina Winterborne had her own reasons for going along with the idea. She wanted to keep her hand in the cookie jar of her daddy's bank account. Despite the vast difference in their motivations, the end result would be the same.

The finalizing of this merger should call for a hefty bonus, Nate decided. Perhaps he'd put that bug in J.R.'s ear as well. After all, it wasn't often that one could claim the coup of the century.

Cal-Borne was going to happen and the whole country would benefit from it. Goodbye OPEC. The Middle East would no longer own the top spot in the oil industry. America would.

Nate could see his picture on the cover of *Newsweek* now. The man of the hour. God bless free enterprise.

He picked up the telephone again and punched in the number for his PI who was keeping an eye on the lovebirds for him. Without getting in the way, Nate wanted to keep tabs on their progress. To ensure all was as it should be.

"Did they sleep together?" he asked when the hushed voice answered.

"Not yet."

Nate couldn't help feeling just a tad bit disappointed. He knew John. Knew him well. If he slept with the woman there would be no turning back. Not that the young man hadn't had one-night stands in the past. He'd had plenty, but John was a man of his word. He would not agree to this merger or this weekend without full commitment. Sleeping with the woman who'd come here to meet the man she was supposed to marry would mean no backing out. John would never go that far and then break the deal.

"But," his P.I. continued, "if it makes you feel any better there was a rather inspired kiss."

Nate's smile returned full force. "Now we're talking. When did this happen?"

"Last night after they returned home from the country club. Our boy had been willing, but the lady ran for cover. Whatever scared her off, she sure as hell enjoyed that kiss."

John knew how to charm the ladies. Nate could feel the victory already. A couple more of those kisses and the little lady would be putty in his hands. Just showed that even a hellion like Regina Winterborne could be tamed by the right man. And John Calhoun was a damn good man. He deserved the best in a life partner. Oddly, despite all he'd learned about the lovely Miss Winterborne before meeting her, Nate had a good feeling about the young woman. She came across as genuinely sincere. And, even stranger, he liked her.

That was saying something.

"Good work," he said to the man waiting on the other end of the line. "Keep me posted."

After replacing the receiver in its cradle, he allowed a pang of guilt. It was underhanded what he was doing, keeping a watch on the courting couple. But Nate only had John's best interest at heart. Regina Winterborne had a reputation for abrupt explosions and impetuous decisions. Who knew? Perhaps she had changed her ways. Whatever the case, Nate wasn't about to leave John on his own with no backup.

The woman, according to the report he'd read on her, was capable of most anything. That she'd impressed him so far didn't mean that Nate trusted her. He'd read too many pages about her famous exploits.

Regina Winterborne could be trouble.

REGINA STOOD at the far end of the aisle in the garishly decorated chapel and stared toward the podium. She wore a lovely beaded white dress. It had cost a fortune in the little boutique next door. But her daddy could afford it. She'd selected all the accessories as well. Shoes, slinky underthings, including a white lacy garter belt, matching purse and a wide-brimmed hat that looked quite elegant with the ensemble. The gloves and lovely bouquet of mixed flowers were the final touches.

The part that bothered her as she hesitated before walking toward her beloved Kevin was the Elvis impersonator standing by his side at the end of the red-carpeted pathway to her eternity. It wasn't bad enough that he needed to lose a good fifty pounds or that he'd donned a wildly embellished white jumpsuit. No, he had to sport the sunglasses and the pork-chop sideburns as well.

Add that to the blue velvet wall covering, the sparkling crystal chandeliers, and the white leather chairs spread on either side of the center aisle for friends and witnesses, and it was entirely repulsive.

Regina had only just realized how repulsive.

The two drunken revelers that had been paid to serve as witnesses to the nuptials sat in intoxicated stupors, beer cans still clutched in their hands.

This wasn't right.

She swallowed tightly and squeezed the neatly wrapped stems in her hands.

Her daddy wouldn't approve. He'd just die when he found out. She glanced briefly at the Priscilla Presley look-alike waiting close by with a loaded Polaroid camera.

Regina blinked and refocused her attention on Kevin. He smiled widely at her, his eyes questioning. She knew he was wondering why she hesitated. They'd blown half his winnings already, but still had enough for a great honeymoon on the beach in Maui.

But then what?

Her daddy's words echoed inside her head. The board would run the company and she would get a measly allowance if she didn't obey his wishes.

A shudder quaked through her.

When he found out—if he didn't know already—

what she'd done, he would be furious. It might even be too late now. He probably had his lawyers drawing up a second codicil to his will at this very moment while she stood in this ungodly Vegas chapel about to be entered into the holy state of matrimony by a man who looked like Elvis.

This just wasn't right.

"I can't do this," she muttered.

Kevin's eyes widened in shock. "Baby, it's okay." He rushed to her, grabbed her by the arms and gave her that puppy-dog look that always won her over. "I love you. We have to get married. It's destiny."

For the first time she took a mental step back and really looked at the man. He was thirty. Hadn't finished college, didn't have a job. All the things her daddy had warned her about came flooding into her head at once. Kevin would amount to nothing. He would keep her happy in bed, when he wasn't running off with his friends. Her gaze narrowed. Oh, yes. That was what had ended their last relationship. Well, that and her father's perpetual interference. And he'd spend her daddy's money like it was going out of print.

She slowly shook her head from side to side. What in the world had possessed her to make this horrible mistake? She could be in Texas right now being wined and dined by a damn good-looking cowboy who had something to offer other than a hyperactive libido and a criminal lack of ambition.

Uneasiness slid through her at the idea. She wanted

to keep her daddy happy but a prearranged marriage might be pushing it. The cowboy would likely want to boss her around. She'd have to live in the middle of nowhere in that godforsaken desert called Texas. Why, they probably didn't even have a Nordstrom's for Christ's sake.

Her brow furrowed in worry. Wait a minute now. Her daddy had said that Dallas had most anything she could ever want, much like Chicago. She'd simply be forced to endure the long ride into the city whenever she wanted to go shopping. Which would be every day she imagined since nothing—absolutely nothing—on a horse ranch could possibly hold her interest for twenty-four hours in a row.

She thrust the flowers in her hand at the man waiting for her to say something. "This isn't destiny, Kevin." She squared her shoulders and glared at him from beneath the brim of her high-priced hat. "It's stupidity. I'm never going to marry you because you have nothing to offer."

With that said she spun on her heel and marched toward the door. She hesitated at the exit for a second and turned back to her jilted lover who stood watching her with his mouth hanging open in shock. "Call me in Texas sometime. We could have ourselves one hell of an affair. But I will never be married to you."

And then she left.

She would hurry back to the suite at the hotel, pack up her newly purchased wardrobe—since the clothes she'd packed previously had gone to Texas—and catch the next flight back to Chicago. It might take a while since it was Sunday and the thousands upon thousands of holiday travelers who'd spent the last forty-eight hours losing their hard-earned money here in Sin City would be headed home, but she would wait patiently. Besides, she needed the time.

It would take some serious time to come up with an acceptable excuse to give her father for her behavior this weekend.

Regina grinned. But she would think of something. She always did. And Daddy always forgave her. He would fix this.

He would take care of everything.

AMY SAT stiffly on the pew as the noonday service wound down. She kept her gaze focused straight ahead. She could not look at the man sitting beside her.

She'd spent the entire morning in her room. Had pretended to be still asleep when he knocked softly around ten. But at eleven she hadn't been able to pretend anymore and she'd spoken to him through the door.

Even with the solid wood panel between them the mere sound of his voice had made her ooze like an ice-cream cone beneath the summer sun. He'd invited her to come to church with him. And for some reason she would never understand she hadn't been able to say no. The underlying plea in his tone had been more than she could bear to deny.

So she'd retrieved the peach-colored skirt and sweater from the closet and hoped it would do. The color looked nice against her tanned skin. She found thankfully that the sandals worked well enough with it. After dancing half the night in those black high heels she'd been positive she would never be able to stand in them today, much less walk.

A quick shower later and she had been ready to prepare for her first Sunday in church since before she'd gone off to college. Somehow though, she lifted a skeptical eyebrow, the lacy white thong and matching bra just hadn't looked suitable for church. But they were all she'd had. Apparently Regina Winterborne preferred the slinky things. Give Amy cotton briefs any day of the week.

As she'd slipped on the ultra-sexy underwear her mind had drifted back to last night and that kiss.

A flush of heat, as much from humiliation as from remembered desire, colored her cheeks, coiled deep in her belly. How could she have come like that from just a kiss? Sure, it had been a long time—two years in fact. But good grief, did she have to explode like a lit firecracker when the man kissed her?

He had to have known.

She closed her eyes even now as humiliation crawled through her all over again. There was no way he could have missed her orgasmic moan and the way she'd stiffened then melted in his big, strong arms.

She'd wondered how on earth she would ever look him in the eye again.

Even with that monumental hurdle looming over her she'd tugged on the sweater and her breath had caught as another epiphany slammed into her skull. Today was the day. She had to tell him the truth.

Fear had blasted her, freezing the heat the memory of his kiss had generated. The fantasy was over. She had to come clean before Mr. Winterborne arrived.

She didn't want John to learn the truth that way.

They'd shared coffee and toast before leaving for the church. Smiling he'd told her that they would have brunch after the service. Then Mr. Beckman had called and announced that her father's arrival would be delayed until Monday.

Amy had almost been relieved. She'd wondered vaguely why Mr. Winterborne hadn't asked to speak with his daughter, but her relief had outweighed all other thoughts.

But Winterborne's postponed arrival didn't change anything. She had to do the right thing.

Sitting in that church, scared to death the roof would fall in on her, she promised herself that she would tell John on the way back to the ranch. She'd never be able to do it in front of his father or Liam or Beckman, so it had to be on the ride home.

Home. She almost laughed out loud. This wasn't her home. He wasn't her fiancé. Nope. John Calhoun and all that came with him belonged to the real Regina Winterborne wherever she might be.

The man beside her shifted, causing his thigh to rub against hers. Amy closed her eyes and forced away the need that arose from even that innocent touch. She had made a terrible, terrible mistake.

Not only was she going to lose her job.

He was going to hate her.

And she was going to be broken-hearted.

Oh yeah. Her heart was involved already. Maybe it had been from the moment she looked into those incredible blue eyes. She shook her head. Quite possibly she'd fallen for him when she saw the photograph attached to the agency's report.

His arm settled around her shoulders and his long, blunt-tipped fingers rested against her arm. Her breath caught as their tips brushed her skin. Remembered heat began to swirl low in her belly. Good heavens, she couldn't be feeling this now…here!

The minister droned on, but Amy didn't really hear him. Her entire being was focused on the hot, hard body next to her. The way his chest pressed against her arm on the left, the feel of his fingers on her right arm. The length of powerful thigh positioned firmly alongside hers.

She admitted defeat and closed her eyes, allowing the remembered feel of his kiss to invade her being. The hungry draw of his lips. The way he'd tasted her, teased her, and then devoured her like a starving man at a forbidden feast. The feel of his body against hers as he'd drawn her closer. And then that little move he'd made, pulling her pelvis against him in oh such an intimate manner.

Longing rushed through her all over again and her feminine muscles throbbed greedily.

Her eyes popped open and she blinked rapidly. She instinctively slowed her breathing and looked side to side without turning her head. She would simply die if anyone were looking at her.

"You okay?" John whispered close to her ear.

Utter humiliation obliterated all else. He'd noticed her heavy breathing or the tension in her muscles. Something. How embarrassing.

She nodded stiffly.

No way could she look at him.

The arm around her shoulder tightened as he protectively pulled her nearer.

His concern touched her.

Made her all the more aware of her deception.

Amy forced her attention on the minister. Lord knew she could use some divine wisdom about now.

WHEN THE SERVICE ended John introduced Gina to more of his neighbors, but he didn't linger long. She seemed to be in a hurry to go. Something was bothering her and he couldn't figure out what it was.

She'd stayed holed up in her room all morning. Then she'd scarcely spoken as they'd shared toast and coffee. He'd thought at one point during the service that she might burst into tears. He sure hoped he hadn't overstepped his bounds last night. He'd thought she wanted that kiss just as much as he did.

In fact, he'd been almost certain that she'd been

moved by it. His gaze instantly sought her in the crowd mingling in the churchyard. That skirt showed off her legs and he liked it a lot. She looked amazing in everything she wore.

She'd left her hair down which drove him crazy with ideas of how he'd love to run his fingers through it. He closed his eyes and allowed last night's kiss to play across the theatre of his mind. He cupped her softly rounded bottom and pulled her intimately to him and he...he was almost sure she'd climaxed or come close. She'd whimpered, tensed, then relaxed against him as if release had come and gone in a red-hot flash.

He opened his eyes and scrubbed a hand over his jaw. Damn. If that was all it took to get her motor running, he could just imagine how she would be in bed. Still, that just didn't fit with what he'd been told about her social life. A woman as experienced as she was supposed to be would have better control than that. A mere kiss wouldn't scorch her to that extent. It just didn't add up.

But then, there was something special between them. Maybe she was as startled by the inferno as he was. Maybe her reaction scared her and that's why she'd stayed in her room this morning.

John shook off that whole line of thinking. They needed to talk some more. To explore those feelings. Now wasn't the time or place.

"Ready?" he asked, moving to her side.

She nodded and smiled but the gesture was forced. That bothered him. He didn't like this other kind of tension between them. The sooner they got home the sooner he could get to the bottom of this. Since her father wasn't arriving until tomorrow, they would have all afternoon and all night. Plenty of time to sort all this out before their fathers interfered.

He didn't want to waste any of the time alone he had left with Gina. He wanted to focus fully on her and where they would go from here.

"John!"

He turned to find Melvin Cook double-timing it toward him. Melvin's ranch bordered the Wild Horse. John immediately thrust out his hand and chastised himself for failing to introduce Gina to his closest neighbor.

"I missed you back there somehow," he offered, certain Melvin was about to rattle his cage about ignoring him.

Melvin pumped John's hand once and smiled at Gina. "I could hardly miss you with this pretty lady at your side."

Gina blushed. The smile she gave the man turned John inside out. He couldn't wait to get her alone. He wanted to see a smile like that directed at him again.

"This is Gina Winterborne. She's visiting from Chicago."

"Ah," Melvin said as he took the hand she offered. "A Yankee. So how do you like Texas?"

"It's wonderful."

Melvin winked. "Better be careful or we'll make a Texan out of you."

She blushed again and John resisted the urge to tell Melvin that he had that part under control. This was one lady he had no intention of letting get away.

"Look, buddy, I hate to ask, but I've got a little problem. A flat tire. Ralph is going to run me over to his gas station to repair it, but the wife and kids—" Melvin shrugged helplessly "—well they don't want to be stuck sitting in the hot sun while I get the repairs taken care of."

"I'll be happy to give them a lift home." John glanced at Gina and smiled reassuringly at her look of concern. "There's plenty of room in that crew cab of mine."

Melvin clapped him on the shoulder. "Thanks, neighbor, I knew I could count on you."

John introduced Gina to Melvin's wife Darlene and their two children, Warren and Connie. After opening Gina's door John opened the rear door of his crew cab truck and assisted Darlene with buckling in the kids. As he did he considered that in a few years he and Gina might have kids of their own. He stole a glance at her and wondered if she had the same goals in mind. Just another thing they had to talk about.

The way she smiled at the children and chatted casually with their mother, John figured she liked kids and had nothing against motherhood. But he needed to know for sure.

He needed a wife in every sense of the word. A broad smile spanned his lips as he climbed behind the wheel and fastened his own seat belt. Judging by her enthusiastic reaction to his kiss last night he had no doubts that they could make it happen.

As he pulled out onto the road he wondered if maybe she was feeling guilty about her *enthusiastic* reaction. Maybe she feared he would hold it against her. There were men who preferred their women less *enthusiastic*. But John wasn't one of them.

If that was her concern she need not worry herself. He liked her reaction just fine. In fact, he loved it. Hoped he could induce it again. Very soon.

He stole a sidelong look at her and made a silent promise that very soon he would show her just how great it could be between them.

Last night had only been an appetizer.

Chapter Eight

The silence was deafening once John had dropped off his neighbors, whose names Amy couldn't even remember.

Dread pooled in her stomach, worry pounded in her brain.

She had to tell him and when she did...

If never seeing him again were the worst of it she might be able to live with that, but it was the shock and hatred she would see in his eyes when reality punched through his disbelief that tore her apart inside.

He would despise her.

For the rest of his life each time he thought of her the memory would be laced with bitterness and ever-hardening hatred.

She covertly swiped at her eyes. But there was no way around it.

As he neared the turn-off to his ranch her anxiety mushroomed to an unbearable level and it was all she could do to hold back the building sobs of regret.

How could she do this in front of Liam? What if

his father showed up? It was Sunday. She remembered him saying that he had brunch with John on Sundays.

"Where's your office?" she blurted, her voice echoing her desperation.

John glanced at her as he slowed to make the turn. "In Dallas. It's—"

"I want to see it…to go there," she urged, the words scarcely squeezing out past the rock of emotion lodged in her throat.

He blinked. "Now?"

She nodded, certain she was beyond speaking at this point.

For one long beat she was sure he intended to try and dissuade her, but then he shrugged as if he could hardly believe what he was about to do. "If that's what you want."

She murmured a thank-you and settled back into the seat. The long ride to Dallas would buy her some time…

As if that would make a difference.

She squeezed her eyes shut and fought the rising tide of tears. She couldn't cry. This was her fault. She had no one to blame but herself.

There was nothing left to do but make it right.

The ninety-minute ride to his office passed without Gina saying a single word. About a dozen times John had started to question her request…to try and get her to tell him whatever was bothering her. But each time, one quick glance at her grim profile had held him silent.

Whatever was bothering her it was serious.

Or was it?

She'd been evasive all morning. Not wanting to talk or even eat, much less go anywhere with him. And now this sudden request to see his office. Was this sort of peculiar behavior what her father had meant when he'd called her petulant?

John hardened his jaw, called himself a damn fool. No, that wasn't right. He knew her. Whatever troubled her today was real. This was no tantrum.

His first guess would be this whole arrangement.

John sighed as he entered the parking garage under the highrise that housed Calhoun Oil's offices. Why had he ever allowed himself to believe that it would be simple? He should have realized that in this day and time a prearranged marriage would never work.

He wondered just how much pressure her daddy had put on her to do this. Had last night's kiss driven home the reality of what she was getting into? Everything had appeared to be going smoothly up until then.

He parked the truck and turned to her, wished he could read her mind. Judging by the troubled expression holding that lovely face hostage, he felt certain her whole world was crashing in on her.

"This is the place," he said with as much cheer as he could inject into his tone.

She nodded and reached for the door handle.

"Gina." He stayed her hand. "Please tell me what's on your mind. Don't lock me out like this."

She looked at him for the first time since they'd left

church. Her eyes were bright with unshed tears and her lips quivered when she spoke, tying his gut into knots. "Just take me inside, okay?"

Knowing a brick wall when he came up against one, he climbed out of the truck and moved around to her door. She'd already gotten out, probably not wanting him to offer assistance of any sort. That would require that they touch and he got the distinct impression that she didn't want him to touch her.

Funny, last night she'd come to life in his arms. What had happened during that kiss to have caused this kind of reaction? To have sent her diving for cover?

Security buzzed them into the lobby.

"I thought I was the only one who had to work today," Carl, the security guard, chortled. "Sure didn't expect to see you, Mr. Calhoun."

"I won't be long," John assured him. "You planning any fireworks tonight?" he asked as he waited for the elevator to arrive. Gina stood beside him saying nothing. She'd hardly managed a smile for Carl. John just couldn't understand the complete turnaround.

"Only the ones on the sports channel," Carl mused. "I'm kicking back tonight."

John didn't keep up with pro ball anymore, but a lot of his friends and colleagues did. He had no idea if anyone was playing. His sole focus was on the woman at his side.

He watched thankfully as the elevator doors glided open just then.

The ascent to the fourteenth floor took mere seconds, but the tension escalated as if a mini eternity had passed.

"This way," he told her when the doors had opened fully.

Amy followed him through reception and past all the smaller offices until they reached the president's office. His office. A large corner space that overlooked the city that he loved almost as much as he did his hometown of Runaway Bay. There was no place on earth quite like Dallas.

It was a city with heart, with roots deep in the soil, kept rich and strong by black crude.

He stopped just inside the door of his office and watched as she moved about the room. Preventing his gaze from dropping to the hem of that cute little skirt and admiring the toned limbs it showed off would have been physically impossible, so he didn't even try.

One small hand drifted over the back of his executive chair as she peered out the wall of windows. Despite the need to know what was going on in her head, he waited. Waited for her to make the first move. Instinct warned him that she needed the space.

She moved again. Crossed the room to study the numerous plaques on the two inner walls. Accolades for Calhoun Oil's environmental efforts. Acknowledgements from the city regarding charitable work and scholarships for up-and-coming young businessmen. And there was that Man of the Year plaque. His secretary had insisted on his displaying the thing.

John worked hard, that was true. But, in his opinion, just because he chose to do good with the money his company earned didn't make him special. It simply made him human.

Gina suddenly turned on him. "So your business files are here in these offices?" She waved her hands magnanimously.

Not certain where she was going with this, he nodded. "That's right."

If anything she looked even more agitated now. He just couldn't figure it out.

She spun on her heel and marched back to his desk, moved behind it and flipped through his appointment calendar.

"And if someone were to search through each and every one of those files—" her gaze locked with his "—what would he find? Any shady activities?" She rolled her eyes and huffed a sound of disbelief. "No, there wouldn't be any, would there? I'll bet you've never even cheated on your tax return."

Her words had somehow prodded him into motion. By the time she finished her last sentence he stood at the corner of his desk, more damn confused.

"What's this about, Gina?" He held her gaze when she would have looked away. "Why'd you hide from me last night and give me the silent treatment this morning?" He threw his hands up in surrender. Something damn close to hurt twisted inside him. She looked so lost…so forlorn. He wanted to reach out to her. To shake her and demand to have some answers. "What'd I do wrong?"

She drew in a deep, ragged breath. "That's just it, John. You didn't do anything wrong. You're perfect. Nothing to hide. No deceptions. Just what you appear to be…the perfect man."

He couldn't take it anymore. The hurt in her eyes ripped him apart. He had to know what this was about. "What do you want me to say to that?" He grabbed her by the shoulders and shook her gently. "Tell me what's going on," he growled, his emotions verging on panic now. He'd only panicked once in his life and that was when his mother had died. Some-how…someway this felt exactly like that. "Where's that woman I held in my arms last night? The one I kissed and who kissed me back…" His eyes went to her trembling lips then. He wanted so badly to kiss her. To make all of this go away.

"She wasn't real…none of it was real."

She'd gone numb. Hated the dramatics, but she just couldn't find the strength to tell him the rest. The confusion, the worry in his eyes squeezed her heart, made her want to break down and cry.

"I think you're wrong about that," he growled savagely.

His mouth came down hard on hers. Amy tried to push him away. Her whole body longed to lean against his…to feel the strength of his arms. But she couldn't let that happen. She had to do this…had to tell him the truth.

She drew back, as far as his hold on her arms would allow, and turned her mouth from his. "There are things you need to know. The truth. I've—"

"I already know all I need to. The past doesn't matter," he urged, breathless.

She shook her head, tried to evade his tempting lips. "It started out as a mistake. I—"

His hands released her arms only to close around her face, holding her still when she would have looked away from the intensity in those beautiful blue eyes. "It doesn't matter. All that matters is this." And then he kissed her again.

Kissed her until she sagged against him, desperation, longing, and desire all warring for her attention.

"No more talk," he whispered against her lips. "Let me show you what's on my mind."

She nodded, completely at his mercy...unable or unwilling to fight the need any longer.

His gaze holding hers in a grip that very nearly frightened her, he shouldered out of his jacket and tossed it aside, then dropped to his knees in front of her. Her breath caught as he shifted her weight against his desk. Good thing, too, her knees suddenly felt too weak to support her. Already her heart hammered in her chest. She felt at once lightheaded and on fire.

She should stop this...

He pushed the hem of her skirt upward and tangled his fingers in the flimsy waistband of her panties. Slowly, surely, his eyes never leaving hers, he dragged the white scrap of lace down her thighs. When it fell haphazardly around her ankles, he urged her legs wider apart. Her eyes went wide as the breath she'd just drawn in promptly evacuated her lungs. His face pressed against her intimately and the moment his mouth moved over her feminine flesh she cried out his name.

Her desperate cry served only as an encouragement to him and the resulting onslaught sent sensation after sensation raining down over her. Her head lolled back and she admitted defeat. She couldn't stop this… whatever tomorrow brought. Here and now she was lost to a fantasy come true…if only for a few hours.

Taking his time he nuzzled and suckled her until every inch of her felt molten with desire. He found that one special place and he drew deeply, nibbled hungrily and then sucked long and hard all over again.

Her inner muscles coiled sharply, tightened with an ache sweeter than any she'd ever known. The intensity of it made the simple act of breathing impossible. She could only grasp the edge of the desk and wait for the spiraling sensation to peak. The coil snapped, wrenching another wanton cry from her and sending ripple after ripple of pleasure cascading through her womb.

When the haze of ecstasy cleared a bit she became aware that he stood over her again…was dragging her sweater up and off. He tugged down the satiny cup of her bra and then that skilled mouth latched onto her breast. That distant ache started all over again. Each tug of his hot, seeking mouth drew on the invisible thread that sent those shivery sensations straight to her feminine core.

His fingers moved over her skin, teasing, tempting, learning every rise and hollow, tweaking the nipple his mouth had just abandoned. He moved to her neglected breast and gave it the same thorough treatment. Laving the pebbled nipple with his wicked tongue. Cupping, rolling the fullness of her breast with his fingers.

Enough. She pulled his face up to hers and offered him her lips. She wanted to feel his mouth on hers…to look into his eyes again and know that this…all of this was for her. This had nothing to do with anything but the two of them. No one would ever be able to take this moment away from her.

His mouth descended upon hers and all thought vanished. There was only the sensation of his firm lips on hers, the hot seek and retreat of his tongue, and the feel of his hands on her skin.

He leaned her back onto his desk, clearing it with one broad stroke of his arm. The ache inside her became more urgent. His hands and mouth weren't going to be enough this time. She needed to touch him…to feel him.

Her fingers tangled with the buttons of his shirt, tugged at his tie. He joined in the effort. Slung off his hundred-dollar tie. Ripped open his designer shirt.

She moaned at the feel of his warm flesh beneath her palms. The vivid male contours of his chest…the slight friction from the scattering of hair there. Her fingers found his waistband and she struggled with the closures there, all the while he kissed her…kissed her everywhere. Her forehead, the tip of her nose, her neck…the swell of her breasts.

He groaned savagely when she pulled him free. Her own sigh of pleasure hissed past her lips as she felt the weight of him in her hands. He was big and hard…perfect.

Dragging her hands away he positioned himself between her thighs and nudged his way to just the right spot. He thrust into her in one smooth stroke. Her eyes closed with the exquisite pleasure of it.

For one space in time they both held completely still, allowing the wondrous sensation to wash over them again and again. When she opened her eyes, his were still closed. She smiled at that, reveling in the idea that he was every bit as affected as she was. Those eyes opened in a heart-stopping show of blue and then he kissed her, softly, sweetly. His fingers found hers and he held her hands in his as he rocked gently inside her.

She kicked free of her panties and wrapped her legs firmly around him as he moved in and out. Slowly. Each drag of his thick sex pushing her closer to the edge.

Over and over he kissed her, whispered sweet words to her, weaving a sensual spell that almost made her believe that this could be real…could last forever.

The first urgent ripples of her release tensed her entire body. She arched to meet his firm thrusts.

Needed him to hurry. To make it happen. To finish this.

As if he could read her mind, he increased the pace. Lifted her bottom for deeper penetration. Once, twice, then the dam broke, sending her over the edge. She clutched at his shoulders, arched her body more intimately against him.

She felt him tense…felt his thrusts become even more urgent. Then he came, sending a rush of heat against her womb. He pumped his hips twice more, draining the last of the release from her as well as him. Then he braced himself on his desk, his body hovering just above hers, those incredible eyes searching hers.

In that moment of utter bliss she suddenly wanted to hear him say her name. She wanted him to know to whom he'd made love…wanted him to connect all these beautiful sensations to her and her alone.

"I don't want this moment to end," she whispered, admitting the fear that burgeoned in her chest. This was all they would ever have and she couldn't bear the thought…

He grinned, stole a kiss then whispered back, "There's always the conference table."

And just like that all else was forgotten.

They made love on the conference table. On the floor of his office. In the executive bathroom. Then they ordered pizza to be delivered.

After they had devoured a double cheese pizza, they made love again.

Not until dark did they return to Runaway Bay. Neither of them spoke during the trip, just like before. But this time it was an amiable silence. Amy relived their hours of lovemaking over and over, her body still hot and quivery.

Judging by the smile on John's face he was doing the same. She closed her eyes and sighed, wishing one last time that this could last.

When he turned onto Stampede Lane reality crashed down around her.

She still hadn't told him the truth.

And time was running out.

This wasn't meant to last.

Chapter Nine

Amy sat on the edge of her bed and listened to the silence. She seemed to be doing a lot of that lately. The silent ride to church. The silence on the way to the Calhoun Oil offices in Dallas. The peaceful, satisfied quiet on the way back to Runaway Bay.

And now the silence that ate away at her like a rapidly moving cancer.

She sucked in a shuddering breath. She'd made a terrible, terrible mistake.

It had started out innocently enough. Not her fault. She wrung her hands together in her lap as she tried to rationalize how this whole thing had happened.

How it had spiraled out of control and turned into…this.

She'd only gone to deliver the report. Regina Winterborne had forced her into this situation.

Nate Beckman had all but wrestled her into the car and refused to listen to her when she tried to tell him he'd made a mistake.

Then there was the report. She looked around the

room. Maybe it was in her suitcase. She couldn't actually remember where it was at the moment. The information accompanying the report had been wrong. She'd taken it too seriously. Proving her worthiness as an agent candidate had been the only thing on her mind. The vivid image of the photograph of John sitting astride that horse flashed before her eyes.

Surely she couldn't have had meeting him in the back of her mind all along? She closed her eyes and shook her head in denial. Yes, the whole idea of the "fantasy" had been intriguing. Being carried off into the sunset by her personal knight in shining armor. But that wasn't why she'd eventually gone along with the mistaken identity.

She'd thought she was doing the right thing. She could prove herself as a Colby agent and save Regina Winterborne from the likes of John Calhoun in the process.

But Regina Winterborne hadn't needed saving. And John was no bad guy. The concerns in the report were unfounded. She was certain of that. Though she wasn't fool enough not to know from a logical standpoint that he could, in fact, be hiding something she hadn't found. What she did know was him. John was one of the good guys. Rich and handsome, yes. But kind and compassionate as well.

Her fingers twisted together as she struggled to hold back the flood of emotions rushing against her composure.

She had allowed this simple mistake to escalate into

an outright tragedy. She had fooled John and his family and friends. She had made a fool out of the agency.

There wasn't much she could do to make it right. Somehow she had to clear up that last part. The steps she had taken had not been authorized by Victoria Colby-Camp. This was not the agency's fault. The responsibility belonged solely to her.

She had to straighten this out. She almost laughed. That was probably too much to hope for. What she had to do was own up to the responsibility to those that it concerned.

She had to tell John the truth.

It wasn't that she hadn't intended to earlier. She had. She'd wanted to tell him this morning but he'd urged her to go to church with him and she just hadn't been able to say no. Then she'd determined to tell him on the way home…

The stress had gotten to her at that point. She'd known what she needed to do but *things* kept getting in the way. She'd demanded that he take her to his office. Had she been thinking or hoping that he would confess to something if she pushed the issue? She was nothing but a desperate woman grasping at straws. He was a good man with nothing to hide. She was the one with the secrets. Coming unglued after they dropped off his neighbors and insisting that he take her to his office had simply been the straw that had broken the camel's back.

At least they'd been alone. She'd had the perfect venue for telling him the truth, for confessing all. This whole thing had started because she wanted to prove he was guilty of shady business dealings.

Then he'd made love to her. Remembered heat flooded her trembling body as her fingers fisted, grasping at her flimsy tether on control. The touch of his mouth, his hands on her body…all of it came rushing back in an instant. She'd given herself completely over to him, hadn't been able to resist.

As wondrous and beautiful as it had been, it was the worst travesty of all. She'd allowed herself to fall in love with a man who didn't even know her real name.

She had allowed him to develop feelings for her as well. But they would change the moment he learned the truth. That reality gave her pause, made her wish there were some other way. Any other way. But there wasn't.

The truth had to come out.

First—she squared her shoulders and dragged in a deep, bolstering breath—she had to talk to Mildred. She didn't want the Colby Agency being blindsided by this. God knew that when she confessed to John she might not be able to think rationally. This part had to be done first.

She picked up the telephone's receiver from the bedside table and dragged it to her lap. Praying Mildred would be at home, she punched in the numbers and held her breath as ring after ring went unanswered. Mildred spent most holidays with her niece. Amy prayed this one would prove an exception.

Finally, to her immense relief, her familiar voice sounded across the miles.

"Mildred, it's Amy. There's something I have to tell you."

To her credit, Mildred waited patiently, reserving comment until Amy had finished her story. It took some time since she broke down occasionally and had to take a moment to pull herself back together.

When she was finished, exhausted by emotion, Mildred said two words Amy least expected. "I see."

Amy laughed. She couldn't help it. Swiping her eyes she forced the amusement triggered by hysteria back into submission. "I'm done for, aren't I?" She shook her head and managed a much-needed breath. "I've hurt John and I've embarrassed the agency."

"Amy," Mildred said with more understanding than Amy had a right to expect, "the notes you found attached to the report were not related to John Calhoun. That was included in the package by mistake. But I can see how you might have concluded exactly what you did. However, it sounds to me like what you've done is hurt yourself. I can hear it in your voice. You keep talking about Mr. Calhoun and the agency, but it's you who's hurting."

Well, that was true. But she had no one to blame but herself. And she should have realized the additional information stuck in with the Calhoun report was a mistake. But she'd been so gung-ho to make a case for herself. To solve the unsolvable. What a screw-up.

"So." She moistened her lips and bit the bullet. "What do I do now?" Actually she knew, but some small part of her prayed that Mildred would have an alternative answer. One that would prove less damaging.

"You tell the truth. Just as you've told me. If John Calhoun is half the man you say he is, then he'll get over it. If he's not, well then, he'll just have to deal with it. That's why the agency has hot-shot attorneys like Zach Ashton."

Amy cringed at the thought of a lawsuit. She could see Beckman contacting an attorney straight away.

"All right," Amy relented. "I'll take care of it. I guess I'll see you in the office on Tuesday."

"Try not to beat yourself up so badly," Mildred offered sympathetically. "Remember, it was a series of unfortunate errors and events, some beyond your control. You did what you thought was right and it simply got out of hand."

Amy swallowed tightly. "Are you going to call Victoria?"

The beat of silence that followed finished shattering any hope Amy had of hanging onto her composure. Tears crested on her lower lashes once more.

Then Mildred surprised her again. "No," she said. "I don't see any point. We won't go that route unless it becomes necessary."

"Thank you," Amy breathed. At least that was something. Another stay of execution. More than she deserved.

When she'd placed the receiver back in its cradle, Amy sat quietly for a while, listening to the silence again, hoping some kernel of wisdom would suddenly pop into her head. But Mildred was right, she had only one recourse.

Moving listlessly, Amy got up and went into the en suite bath to run herself a deep, hot tub of water. She hadn't been able to bear the thought of washing away the essence of John at first. She'd needed to know that he lingered on her skin. She could hold her sweater to her face and smell his enticing scent even now.

Before slipping into the warm depths of the water, she closed her eyes and allowed those hours in Dallas to whisper through her mind. Then, when her courage had solidified, she faced reality and slipped into the tub, washing away the sweet past they had shared and all hope of any future.

JOHN ROAMED the yard. Checked the horses. Wished again that he'd gotten another dog after Champ died. He shook his head and dropped onto the open tailgate of his truck. How long had it been since he'd thought of that dog?

God, years.

He'd told himself he was too busy for a dog nowadays. He spent a great deal of time in Dallas, and when he was on the ranch there was a tremendous amount of responsibility waiting. Liam would love the company, he mused. Maybe he should get another one.

Of course he'd need to run that by Gina. If this was

going to be her home, she had input as well. A frown wormed its way across his brow. For the first time since he'd met the pretty lady, real worry twisted in his gut. What if she didn't want to marry him? What if she didn't want any of this?

When Nate and his father had first approached him with this harebrained scheme he'd flat out said no. But then, he'd thought about it and he'd known, from a financial standpoint, it was damn brilliant. He'd told himself that as long as the woman was willing to be the kind of wife he wanted, it could work. They could learn to love each other.

And then she'd waltzed into his life and all that had blown to hell and back. She was nothing like what he'd expected. The beauty, he'd anticipated. But there was far more to this woman than mere looks. She had a depth that startled him. She was passionate and funny and sweet. A smile tugged at the corners of his mouth. And, despite the hours of lovemaking this afternoon, he wanted her still. Could make love to her over and over this very night. Was certain he would never grow tired of feeling her come apart in his arms.

He hadn't actually expected them to reach the point of lovemaking this weekend, though he'd heard otherwise. The fact was, she hadn't felt like the experienced vixen he'd believed her to be from the reports he'd read. She felt…almost virginal. Tight as a fist. So soft and vulnerable. Two things he wouldn't have associated with a more worldly woman. She'd allowed him to lead, though she'd followed readily, she hadn't tried to take control. Another indication that she didn't have nearly the sexual experience he'd been led to believe.

That startled him just a little. Oh, it pleased him rightly enough, but it scared him, too. Hell, what was he saying? It didn't scare him, it overpowered him. He hadn't just made love to her. He'd fallen *in* love with her.

Now there was a first.

John had never fallen head over heels for any woman, certainly not in the span of forty-eight hours. But there it was. He glanced toward the light gleaming from her bedroom window. He cared deeply for her, couldn't imagine his life without her.

How ironic was that?

His cagey father had pleaded with him to go along with this whole thing…had worked overtime to convince him. Finally John had given in, having no idea that the woman herself would steal his heart before he could see the first step of the scheme through.

Headlights bobbed as a vehicle meandered down Stampede Lane toward the house. Once the truck stopped near the house, the exterior lights revealed the make and owner.

"Speak of the devil," John muttered.

His dad climbed out of the truck, caught sight of John and sauntered in his direction.

"Enjoying the moonlight?" J.R. gestured to the full moon hanging low in the sky.

John laughed. Actually it was the first time he'd

noticed. He'd been too caught up in his thoughts to be aware of anything else. "Yeah," he lied. "I'm a sucker for full moons."

J.R. hefted himself on to the tailgate next to his son. "Where's that sweet little filly? Liam said the two of you didn't show up for the fine brunch he'd prepared."

For the first time today John considered that he and Gina had taken off for Dallas without telling a soul. He sighed. Damn.

"Last-minute change of plans."

J.R. leaned toward him and sniffed like an old 'coon dog. "Yeah, I can smell just how much fun you had."

John scrubbed a hand over his face. He hadn't bothered with a shower. The smell of sex as well as the subtle scent of roses still lingered on his skin…his clothes. Leave it to his old man to pick up on that right away.

"It's what you wanted, isn't it?" John demanded defensively. Was he supposed to feel guilty for making "it" happen?

"That's not fair," J.R. grumbled.

John just shook his head. "It's not fair, but it is what you wanted." Now he was angry. It didn't make total sense but he'd lost the last of his control. "You wanted us to hit it off, to seal this big deal with a wedding. Bedding the woman had to be expected."

His father looked away. "That's a little crude, son."

Now the man felt guilty! And John knew the reason. It had all felt different when they had talked about some unknown person…some female suspected of being wild and wicked, thoughtless and selfish. But it was different now. They'd met the woman and she was sweet and…innocent. Yes, dammit, innocent. She was kind and thoughtful.

This was the woman J.R. and Nate had decided would be John's wife for better or worse. Hell no, for the money.

Fury unleashed inside him and he bolted to his feet. He glowered at his father. "This is what you wanted and you have the nerve to chastise me with that tone about having sex with the woman. Is that right, Mr. I-see-a-different-lady-friend-every-night?"

J.R. slid off the tailgate and matched his stance. "Don't take that tone with me, son. I'm still your old man whether you like my business tactics or not."

John felt immediately contrite. Took a breath. He braced his hands at his waist and fought for calm. "I'm sorry. You're right. I was out of line."

J.R. shook his head. His shoulders sagged with defeat. "No, I'm the one who was out of line. We planned this whole strategy. All three of us, Nate, Winterborne and me. We planned it like the two of you were assets, not people…not our children." He shook his head again. "It was wrong. I didn't stop and think what it would cost you…what it would do to you." He released a shuddering breath. "And I damn sure didn't think what it would cost her. She's a good woman, son. I hope we haven't made a mistake."

John knew what he meant. He was talking about the

fact that John had gone the ultimate distance. He'd made love to her. J.R.'s honor was stinging right now. What the hell? John's was doing the same thing.

It shouldn't have happened this way. Love and family should be above propositions and negotiations. Neither of them should ever have allowed any of this.

John reached out to his dad, squeezed his shoulder. "You can rest easy on that score, Dad. There's no mistake. She's the one for me."

J.R.'s face split into a relieved grin. "I'm sure glad to hear that 'cause Liam and I had already decided she fit right in with this family."

John laughed. Great. Liam and his father had decided. "That's good," he said and meant it. He looked toward her window again. "She still has a few reservations I think," he said as much to himself as to his father.

J.R. followed his gaze. "You don't think she feels the same way you do?"

John rolled over in his mind the little signs of misgivings he'd noted. "No, that's not the problem. I think she feels very much the way I do on one level, but there's something that's causing her to hold back. She tried to explain that there was more she needed to tell me." He shrugged. "Some truth she thought I should know."

"The gossip about her past maybe?" J.R. offered. "I don't believe any of it at this point."

"Maybe. I don't know." His eyes locked with his father's once more. "But I can guarantee you one thing, there isn't a force on this planet that will prevent me from spending the rest of my life with that pretty lady.'' He turned back to stare toward her room. ''Whether she realizes it yet or not, she's mine. I won't let her get away.''

AMY COMBED OUT her damp hair and studied her reflection in the mirror. It was the first time she'd really looked at herself since this whole thing started. Nothing had changed on the outside. She still looked like the same old girl she'd been on Friday while flipping through the latest glamour magazine.

How many times had she fantasized about the perfect man—the one for her—who would burst onto the stage of her existence and make her life all that it should be and more. But that hadn't happened. She hadn't met the first guy who even remotely resembled the hero of her heart…her imaginary lover.

So she'd done what any intelligent girl who was a romantic at heart would do, she'd committed herself to her work. Focused on her career and promised herself on those lonely nights with nothing but a good book and a cup of hot chocolate to keep her warm that her turn would come.

She would be the heroine in the latest novel she'd read. The one who got the guy and who lived happily ever after.

And what do you know, she had met the perfect man. The one accurately described in the article. The only one who had made her heart pound with anticipation and her womanhood sing with joy. John Calhoun was that man. He was all she'd ever hoped for.

But she was a lie.

She stared at the woman in the mirror. She'd had her taste of heaven, her fantasy come true, and now it was over. Ruined by her own stupidity.

A soft knock at the door jerked her from her Amy-bashing session. It would be him, no question. She laid the brush aside and surveyed her emotional state to see if she had the courage to go ahead and break it to him now.

Nope.

That much courage likely didn't exist in a mere mortal.

She glanced at the clock as she moved back into her bedroom. Almost ten. It was too late at night to deliver her revelation anyway. God knew she'd need a ride out of here and she doubted she could get one tonight, much less a flight back to Chicago. Come to think of it, she didn't even have her purse. Renewed panic clawed at her throat. How would she board a plane? She didn't have any ID, no credit card, no cash. Nothing.

Shaking her head, she pulled the robe more tightly around her and summoned what little courage she did have. Her fingers wrapped around the door knob just as the second knock rasped on the closed wooden panel.

She opened the door and peered up into the mesmerizing blue eyes of the man who would soon hate the very sight of her. Try as she might a smile wouldn't form on her lips.

"It's late I know," he said, his voice gentle in spite of the thick underlying emotions she heard.

She had done this to him. Selfish, thoughtless wretch she was. And all this time she'd worried that Regina Winterborne would be bad for him.

She was the evil one here.

"That's okay," she managed to say in a somewhat normal voice. Her heart rate had already accelerated simply looking at him. Her mind started to list his numerous assets and skills: his ability to make her come with the mere flick of his tongue in just the right place or the feel of his masterful hands gliding over her skin.

"You rushed inside so quickly when we arrived I didn't get to say good-night." The hopeful smile tilting the corners of that sexy mouth almost obliterated the last vestiges of her control.

They'd been back at the ranch for almost two hours. Apparently she wasn't the only one who'd needed to screw up some courage.

Nothing she said at this point would be right…it would only make bad matters worse. "John, there are things I have to tell you." She looked up into those devastating eyes. "I'm not who you think I am. I tried to tell you before but—"

He pressed a finger to her lips, halting her confession. He dropped his hand to hers, entwining their fingers. "It doesn't matter. I know you don't want to believe it's that simple, but it is.'' He sighed. ''Hell, I can't even believe it myself. Nothing else matters.''

She couldn't let him say the words. As crazy as it sounded, every instinct warned her that he was about to tell her that he loved her. What she'd already done to him would be humiliating enough. She couldn't allow him to do this. The blow to his ego would be too much. It was bad enough that his heart would suffer the damage. But he was a man, he wouldn't want it to show. He wouldn't want her to know how badly she had injured him.

She'd learned a lot about men and what made them tick from magazines. Not to mention she worked with a dozen handsome men every day. No matter how strong, how death-defying they were, their egos were still tender.

''Gina, I—''

Before he could finish his statement, she grabbed him by the shirt front and pulled his mouth down to hers. She kissed him hard and fast, unleashed all the pent-up emotion inside her, then she released him.

''Good night, John.''

She closed the door before he could respond. Leaning against it she squeezed her eyes shut and fought the dizzying hurricane of emotions she'd let loose.

For one long minute he remained just on the other side of the door. Finally he moved away. Not until well after that did she manage the strength to push away from the door.

This wasn't going to work. Every time she tried to

tell him he stopped her. Time had already run out as far as she was concerned. There was only one thing left to do. She would write him a note.

She winced at the thought that leaving a note made her a coward. But it wasn't entirely her fault. She'd tried to tell him. Tried repeatedly. She couldn't let anything else get in the way of his learning the truth. Edgar Winterborne would be here by noon tomorrow and she couldn't bear John to learn the truth that way.

Determined to get this done, she sneaked from her room and went in search of pen and paper. She would get up really early tomorrow morning and ask Liam to drive her into town. From there she would figure out what to do next. The note would be left on the kitchen table for John. It was the cowardly way, but at least it would get the job done.

And it would save them both from having to endure the hurtful words launched like spears in the heat of emotion.

It was the best solution for all concerned. One day he would appreciate it. She already did.

REGINA WINTERBORNE paid the taxi driver and hurried the rest of the way down the drive. She hadn't wanted him to pull all the way up to the house for fear of waking her father. It was well after midnight and he would be in bed. All she had to do was sneak around to the back door and slip inside. She had a key hidden there for just such an occasion.

Moving quietly across the manicured lawn, she

reached the rear terrace garden and fumbled in the flower pots until she found where she'd hidden that key. She hadn't used it in so long she'd almost forgotten where it was. After dusting the dirt from it, she felt for the lock, unable to see in the darkness.

The door opened with a minimal creak and she eased it open. When she was certain the alarm had not been set, she relaxed. She knew the code of course, but her father would hear the beep that accompanied the opening of a door whenever it was armed.

Exhaling the breath she'd been holding, she quietly closed and locked the door, then tackled the stairs. She knew just which treads groaned under the weight of a footfall. When she'd reached the upstairs landing she moved more quickly on the carpeted floor.

Inside her room she locked the door and hurried to the bathroom. All she wanted right now was a hot bath to wash away the stench of a long flight in coach. Then a few hours of beauty rest would be in order.

She needed the sleep to build up her strength. The whirlwind weekend in Vegas had been exhausting. She also needed to work up her courage. It would take all the strength and courage she could muster to face the wrath of her father. He'd had two days to build up a raging fury. She imagined that he's had a full search party out looking for her within minutes of hearing she'd failed to meet the Calhoun party—had left another woman to face the music, so to speak. Of course he would be worried sick as well. But as soon as he knew she was safe…

All hell was going to break loose.

Chapter Ten

"Good morning, Liam."

The man started and whipped around from the pan of sizzling bacon. "Morning," he drawled, clearly surprised to see her up at daybreak. But the startled look on his face evacuated abruptly when he saw the packed bag sitting at her feet. "You leaving us this morning, Miss Gina?" That cunning gaze narrowed during the five seconds it took her to summon the courage to answer his question.

"Yes." The solitary word reflected the numerous emotions grappling for control inside her. She'd hardly slept at all last night. She kept imagining the disappointment and hatred she would see in John's eyes when he learned the truth.

There was no way to stop it from happening. She wasn't Regina Winterborne. This was not her life. Her life was back in Chicago as Amy Wells, personal assistant with no future prospects where romance was concerned. She'd allowed this ruse to take place, ultimately stealing a chunk of time from someone else's life. She was a thief...a voyeur. Nothing more.

Liam's suspicious expression seemed to deflate in the face of her immense sadness. "Can't even stay for breakfast?" he tempted.

She shook her head. "It would mean a lot to me if you could take me into town. I'll figure out something from there." The burn of tears raged at the backs of her eyes, but she blinked it away. She had to be strong. This was her fault...no one else's.

Liam nodded with understanding. "Just let me get this—" he gestured to the stove "—under control and we'll be off."

Amy left her bag in the kitchen and made her way to the entry hall. She listened to make sure the coast was clear before crossing to the table near the front door. She'd leave the letter here by his keys. He always tossed them onto the table whenever he came in. She propped the sealed envelope where he couldn't possibly miss it, then hurried back to the kitchen. John had been in the shower when she'd come down. She'd listened at his door to be sure. Any minute now he would likely come downstairs.

When he did, she wanted to be gone.

Like the coward she was.

JOHN SLIPPED the final button on his shirt into its closure then reached for his hat. Something that felt like utter bliss bloomed on his lips in a wide smile.

He'd made up his mind. He wasn't letting Gina go

back to Chicago without a decision to ponder. Today, before her father's arrival, he would officially ask her to be his wife. No way would he let her go back after they'd made love without knowing the full scope of his intentions, business merger be damned.

The kind of happiness he hadn't even dreamed of hoping for under the circumstances was going to be his. He'd already put in a call to a friend who owned the jewelry store in Runaway Bay. It didn't matter that the store was closed for the holiday, John would take Gina and let her pick out anything her heart desired. A ring that not only reflected her beauty but that would serve as a reminder of his love.

In fact, he couldn't think of a better way to start the day than with this kind of surprise. John reached for the telephone, anticipation humming inside him. This would be a day neither of them would ever forget.

IT TOOK Liam a full ten minutes to get things "under control." Amy had suffered a thousand deaths during every second of every excruciatingly long minute.

Finally he was ready to drive her into town. "I'll just put this in the truck," he said, hefting her borrowed bag.

Amy nodded, the movement more a stiff twitch. Fear pounded in the back of her skull as she followed Liam through the back door and out to his truck. Once the bag was loaded she released the breath she'd been holding.

It was almost over.

The sound of gravel crunching under tires jerked her gaze toward the long drive leading to the house. An SUV, big and black, pulled up right behind Liam's truck. Amy's heart rushed into her throat.

God, she was too late.

Please don't let this be Mr. Winterborne, she prayed.

Nate Beckman climbed out of the vehicle and strode straight up to her. She couldn't read his unyielding, poker-faced expression. Fear held her speechless, her pulse tripping madly.

"You must come with me," he said succinctly as he took her by the arm.

Amy wanted to argue but she couldn't manage the necessary physical or mental ability. As Beckman opened the passenger-side door of his SUV, she glanced helplessly back at Liam. He just stood there looking almost as helpless as she did.

When Beckman backed away from Liam's truck Amy's heart abruptly slid back into her chest and started to pound frantically. As she watched, Liam shrugged and ambled back toward the house.

Dazed and confused she shifted her focus to the driver. What was going on? Did he know already? Where was he taking her? Maybe he wanted to get her away from John before he let her have it. If she were lucky he'd take her back to that private airfield and put her on that same jet she'd arrived in and send her back to Chicago.

Once they reached the main road he pointed the

vehicle toward Runaway Bay and settled in for the drive without a word. Amy stared at him, wondering how he could hold whatever he was thinking inside. Why didn't he rant at her? Demand answers? Anything! The silence was more than she could bear.

"Where…" She cleared her throat of the emotion swelling there. "Where are we going?"

She had a right to know that, didn't she? He couldn't just…

Her eyes suddenly rounded in horror. What if he was taking her to the sheriff or chief of police? Could she be arrested for pretending to be someone she wasn't?

A new kind of fear reared its ugly head. The last thing she wanted to do was embarrass the Colby Agency.

Beckman cut her a quick look. "Relax. We'll be there soon."

"But I—"

"That's all I can tell you," he interrupted without even sparing her a glance. A smirk suddenly marred his profile. "You shouldn't be surprised."

She wasn't. Not really. She leaned more fully into the seat and turned to stare out the window at the passing landscape that had become so familiar to her. Beckman would want to protect John from the ugliness of confrontation. He'd likely already discussed the issue with Edgar Winterborne and had decided to intercede on John's behalf. When she was out of the picture he would return to the ranch and break the news to the Calhoun family. Amy felt another wave of sadness. She hated disappointing J.R. almost as much as she did hurting John. Neither of them would ever forgive her.

Thank God she'd written the note. If John bothered to read it at least he would know how sorry she was.

After a few minutes of seemingly driving in circles, Beckman parked his SUV in an alleyway behind a row of what appeared to be offices or shops. She couldn't tell from the backside. Another flood of anxiety crashed over her already raw nerves.

"Why are we here?" Her gaze zeroed in on the driver's.

He looked at her knowingly. "You should know the answer to that."

Her heart rate climbed so rapidly she felt light-headed. "Is he here?"

"Of course he's here," Beckman said in that same condescending tone he'd used with her the first time they met.

She moistened her lips and gulped in a lungful of air. "What does he want from me? It's—"

"Just a simple answer," he said, cutting off the hysterical tirade she'd been about to launch.

Resigned to her fate, she nodded.

Beckman slipped from the vehicle, smoothly rounded the hood and opened her door. She climbed out awkwardly, her movements jerky. Her body didn't want to cooperate with the orders her foggy brain issued. Whatever the man had to say to her, she had no choice but to face it. She had allowed this to happen. Had assumed his daughter's identity, he had a right to demand an answer.

Abruptly a new possibility barged into her racing thoughts. What if he held against her the fact that she had known what his daughter was up to in Vegas in time for it to be stopped? That's what she should have done. She should have demanded that Beckman listen to her in the first place and she should have told him everything.

Just look at all the damage that had resulted from her stupidity.

Beckman opened the back door of one of the buildings and ushered her inside.

He paused near a small cluster of folding chairs stationed in the short corridor. "Sit." He motioned to the chair. "He'll be ready to see you in a moment."

She didn't bother responding. What was the point? Forcing her knees to bend, she settled on the edge of the nearest seat, praying for a bolt of lightning to end her misery, or for an earthquake to split the ground open so that it could swallow her up. Anything to get this over with. Beckman entered a door to her right, closing it soundly behind him.

What felt like minutes but was probably only seconds passed as her anxiety climbed higher and higher. She kept shifting in the chair, looking both ways as if expecting an attack from one side or the other. She listened…strained to hear any kind of sound. Nothing. It was as if she were alone.

The same door Beckman had gone through opened once more. John stepped into the corridor, his gaze instantly seeking hers.

Equal measures of relief and uncertainty grabbed her by the throat. A part of her was so thankful to see him, but another part, the more rational side, realized that this was the moment she had dreaded.

This was the end.

"I want you to understand that I have to do this," he said softly as he settled into a chair next to her.

She managed a shaky smile. "I'm sorry," she told him, holding back the tears, determined not to make this any messier than it already was.

He frowned, looked strangely confused. "Why would you be sorry?" He took her hand in his. "I know this is sudden, but I know it's the right thing to do." He put his free hand against his chest. "I can feel it right here."

Now Amy was the one confused. She shook her head and tried to reason out what he meant. "I don't understand."

He smiled and her heart stuttered. "I'm asking you to consider being my wife and the offer has absolutely nothing to do with the merger of our two companies. If that doesn't work out, it doesn't work out." He nodded his head resolutely. "I decided once and for all last night that I wasn't going to let that be the deciding factor in our happiness. This—" he looked directly into her eyes "—is about us."

Stunned, she could only stare at him.

"Now." He stood, pulling her up with him. "Come with me."

Amy followed, too dumbfounded to do otherwise.

They went through the same door Beckman had entered what felt like forever ago. Amy blinked and looked again, certain she couldn't be seeing what she thought she saw.

John waved his arm to indicate the room at large. "Take your pick. Whatever you want." He smiled down at her with love in his eyes. "I love you, Gina, but I don't expect you to make a decision now. I want you to take the engagement ring of your choice back home with you today and give my proposal as much consideration as you need to. And when you're ready, you can give me your answer."

She wanted to throw her arms around him and tell him that she loved him too and that she didn't have to think about it. She would be happy spending the rest of her life being his wife.

But he hadn't asked Amy Wells to marry him. He hadn't even told *her* he loved her. This was all for Regina Winterborne and she wasn't even here.

John chuckled. "Well, don't look so depressed," he scolded, his tone teasing.

Something buzzed in the ensuing silence. Beckman, who stood not far away along with another man, reached into his jacket pocket. "Excuse me," he mumbled as he withdrew his cell phone. He hurried to the far side of the room and quietly answered the call.

Amy stood frozen like a statue, her heart breaking, the tears that had been threatening all morning rising like a tidal wave behind her lashes.

JOHN didn't get it.

She stared up at him as if she might burst into tears any moment. What had he done wrong?

Then suddenly he knew.

She didn't feel the same way.

God almighty. What a fool he was. His expression fell. He'd obviously misread everything. The way she looked at him. The enthusiastic, almost desperate, way she'd made love with him. How could he have been that wrong?

"John…I'm not…who you think I am," she said brokenly.

"John." Nate came up beside him and offered his cellular phone. "I think you're going to want to take this."

John blinked, torn between demanding to know what she meant and asking what the hell Nate thought was so damn important that it couldn't wait until he'd wrung a more enthusiastic reaction to his proposal of marriage from the woman he loved.

Too overwhelmed to make a proper decision he snagged the phone and jammed it against his ear. "What?" he barked.

"What the hell have you done?"

It took a moment for John to recognize the voice through the confusion and growing disillusionment currently fogging his brain. "Winterborne?" The enraged voice had certainly sounded like Edgar Winterborne.

"What did you do to send my daughter running back here?" the man demanded. "She's locked herself in her room and refuses to come out."

This was crazy. "What do you mean she came running back there?" John demanded back at him. That was impossible. He was looking at her. He blinked again. And she looked as if the whole world had suddenly fallen in on her. Why had his proposal caused such a devastating effect? If she *really* didn't feel the same way all she had to do was say no. But he still couldn't believe that his instincts about her...about them...had been that far off the mark.

"What do you think I mean, you son of a bitch? She's devastated. What did you do to her?"

A short, strained laugh burst from John. "Mr. Winterborne, your daughter is standing right in front of me. The only damn thing I've done that seems to have unsettled her is ask her to marry me."

"I don't know what you think you're doing, Calhoun," Winterborne warned. "Maybe you're on drugs or you've lost your mind, but *my* daughter is here with me. She's in her room." Some of the fury seemed to drain from his voice. "I can't get her to open the door. I can hear her weeping in there, but she refuses to let me in. I don't know what to do."

The sincerity in the man's words slammed into John's gut like a battering ram. He was telling the truth. There was no reason for him to lie in the first place. His daughter was there, in Chicago, with him, crying her eyes out over Lord only knew what.

His focus cleared and his eyes locked on the woman standing before him. "I'll get back to you," he muttered and closed the phone, almost crushing it in his fist. "Who are you?" he asked the stranger staring back at him.

"John, I hope you'll let me explain."

"Oh, that would be helpful," he fired back with a choked laugh. Why hadn't he seen this coming? The signs had been there. "Somebody needs to fill me in on what the hell is going on!"

This was the moment Amy had dreaded. Not facing the truth. Not accepting the responsibility for what she'd allowed to happen. What she hadn't been able to bear the thought of was the hurt and confusion in his eyes. Emotions she knew would quickly change to anger and then hatred.

She sucked in a ragged breath and steeled herself. "It started out as a mistake." Taking her time, her throat very nearly closing with emotion at times, and her mouth so dry she could scarcely form the words, she told him how she had come to be here posing as Regina Winterborne.

When at last she'd finished her full confession, unbelievably without breaking down completely, she didn't ask him to forgive her because she didn't deserve it. She had only one thing to ask of him.

"Please don't hold my poor judgment against the

agency,'' she pleaded. ''This was my idea completely. Victoria doesn't even know I'm here. Had I delivered the report as instructed, the mistake would have been cleared up immediately and none of this would have happened.'' When he continued to stare mutely at her, she licked her dry, trembling lips and added, ''I accept full responsibility for everything.''

He gave his head a little shake, the frown of confusion deepening. ''You let me believe you were Regina Winterborne all this time...'' He searched her face, looking for some sort of reasonable explanation she knew he wasn't going to find. Reason had nothing to do with any of this. ''We...'' He shook his head, with more conviction this time. ''And still you let me believe a lie.''

God, here it came. ''Yes,'' she admitted. He didn't have to say the words. She knew he was referring to their time in Dallas at his office...the lovemaking.

He swiped a hand over his face, suddenly looking anywhere but at her. ''I can't believe you...this just isn't possible.'' He stared hard at her. ''How could you do this?''

There it was, the bitterness that would harden into hatred.

''I was wrong. I didn't know—''

''I'll tell you how she could do it,'' Beckman roared. ''She saw the opportunity to snag herself a rich husband and she went for it,'' he accused brutally. ''That's why you asked me all those questions on the flight. You were working out your strategy.'' He shook his head and then stabbed a finger at her. "You're a gold digger. That's what you are!"

Amy's entire being shattered at his hurtful accusations. Despite her fierce hold on her emotions, a single, humiliating tear rolled down her cheek. She swung her head side to side in denial of his horrible accusation. "No," she argued. "That's not what happened."

Beckman glowered at her. "That's exactly what happened," he snapped. "I'll see that you're dismissed immediately by your employer and—"

"That's enough," John cut him off, his tone harsh.

"I won't let her get away with doing this to you, John," Beckman assured him. "I'm certain the Winterbornes will want to file a suit of their own." He turned back to Amy. "You're in very serious trouble, Miss…Miss…whoever you are."

"I said *enough*," John warned, his voice lethal.

Nate seethed in silence, but his glower remained in full force.

John gathered his scattered wits and allowed his gaze to settle on…the woman who waited silently for whatever was to come next. His newly recovered composure almost slipped from his grasp as he watched a solitary tear slide down her cheek. But the idea that she had lied to him, let him believe in a lie…fall in love with a lie, quickly shored up his crumbling resolve.

"There will be no suit," he said as much to Nate as to her. "Or any contact with your employer."

When Nate would have blurted his argument, John silenced him with an uplifted hand.

"I can't speak for the Winterbornes," he went on, "but I can speak for myself. I damn sure don't want this turned into a more public spectacle than it already is."

She nodded stiffly.

He squeezed his eyes shut for a second, unable to keep looking at her and keep an objective attitude. How could this be? How could all that he'd believed in and fallen for this weekend have been a lie? When he could look at her again, he continued, "I'll have the pilot ready the jet to take you back to Chicago."

Her slender shoulders sagged with relief. "Thank you," she said softly as she took a shaky swipe at her eyes.

She was trying desperately to hold it together. That part he didn't understand. He would have thought she'd have used the tears and theatrics as a plea for sympathy. But she didn't. John tamped down the respect that instantly arose.

"Before you go, I want to know your name." When she'd related her story, she kept saying *I* or *me*. Apparently she'd been so upset she hadn't remembered to identify herself.

"Amy," she said quietly. "My name is Amy Wells."

The name filtered through the emotional chaos in his head. Oddly, he mused, the name fit her. But that point was moot. She'd been out to prove herself. She'd had a hidden agenda for every moment they'd shared together. The memories of their lovemaking flashed one after the other before he could stop it. How could she have faked that? Every touch…every kiss had felt so damn real.

He gritted his teeth and reminded himself that it had all been a lie. He wanted to shake her, to demand something more than the explanation she'd given. But what good would that do? Their weekend together would still be a lie.

"I'm calling the pilot," Nate said as he moved toward the door. "I'll take *Miss Wells* to the airfield."

She flinched at the savagery of his tone.

John wondered at that. How could a woman capable of carrying out this kind of deception be pained by something as harmless as an unkind or facetious tone?

"There's just one thing I have to know before you leave," he said when she started to follow Nate, the words out of his mouth before he had time to consider the wisdom of pursuing the issue. He must be a glutton for punishment.

She paused and turned back to him, those big brown eyes wide with trepidation, still liquid with unshed emotion. Despite all that he knew she'd done she still managed to look innocent and vulnerable. Clearly he had lost his mind. But he had to know the answer to this one question.

Emotion welled in his chest. "Was even a single moment of what we shared real to you?"

For three trauma-filled beats he was certain she wasn't going to answer…then she spoke.

"Not a single moment," she told him, the words scarcely a whisper but wielding more hurt than he'd imagined possible to feel. "*Every* moment was real."

Then she walked away.

By the time her answer had sifted through the hurt and anger exploding inside him, she was gone.

Chapter Eleven

Every moment…

Amy curled up on the sofa and pulled the ancient afghan tighter around her neck, trying to ward off a chill that had nothing to do with the temperature in her tiny Chicago apartment.

She should be at work. But Mildred had insisted she stay home and lick her wounds. Which was exactly all she felt like doing. Amy drew her knees tighter to her chest and rested her cheek atop them. She needed sleep but couldn't make her mind shut down.

All night long she had lain perfectly still in her bed in hopes of falling asleep but it hadn't helped. The voices and images wouldn't hush…wouldn't go away. She kept seeing John's face when he'd asked her if any of it had been real. The anger…the hurt. Pain she had caused.

She'd told him the truth before walking away. *Every moment* had been real. Hard as she tried to push the memories away, they reeled through her mind as well, unhindered by her every attempt to make them go away. The ride they'd taken on the ranch, the picnic…that first kiss. Making love. His heart-wrenching proposal. It was all indelibly ingrained upon her heart, in her mind.

Now she knew what it felt like to live the fantasy…and to lose it. If she'd had any idea losing would hurt this much, she'd never have taken the risk. How did one recover? The idea of ever falling in love with anyone else was out of the question. Her heart belonged to a man who would never be hers.

New plans for a getaway with the real Regina Winterborne were probably already underway. Beckman would be on top of that for sure. And John…

She sighed. Well, he would simply do what was best for his company. She understood that about him now. He loved his father and his company. The responsibility to do what was right for both weighed heavily upon his shoulders. He wouldn't let either down, even if it meant spending the rest of his life with the wrong woman.

Amy shuddered at the thought of John and Regina together.

In her heart, John Calhoun would always belong to her.

A belated realization punched Amy in the stomach, making her breath catch.

They hadn't used a condom. Fear curled around her. How could she have let that happen? She'd always been so careful. She made an exasperated sound at the thought. Yeah, all three times she'd been really cautious, ensuring the use of protection in each incidence.

A new kind of anxiety clawing its way up her spine, she quickly did the calculations for her monthly cycle. A sigh hissed past her lips when she determined that most likely she was safe on that score.

Still, the fleeting thought of having John's child sent a little tingle through her.

"Idiot!" she muttered.

Yes, she was an idiot for thinking even for a second that she would love to have his child whether she had him or not. That wouldn't be good for her and it sure wouldn't be good for the child. Life was tough enough, a child needed every advantage from the beginning. Starting off with even one disadvantage, especially one as big as not having a father, would not be a good thing.

What was wrong with her? Here she was worrying about motherhood when the prospect of marriage was zilch. She should be at work. That's all there was to it. As if she didn't have enough to worry about, her mind went immediately to the other possibilities related to not using protection. She closed her eyes and forced the dreadful thought away.

Her phone rang, startling a little yelp out of her.

For just one second she allowed herself to hope it might be him. That he'd realized he couldn't live without her and that she should come back to Texas and pick out that ring after all. She shook off the foolish dream and scrambled to her feet, letting the afghan fall to the cool hardwood floor.

She was no Cinderella and John was no fairy-tale prince. This was real life, he wouldn't be showing up at her door to whisk her away to his castle after she'd lied to him.

One look at the caller ID unit and her heart skipped a beat.

The office.

Oh, no.

What if the Winterbornes had complained to Victoria? What if she was about to be fired?

Amy stiffened her spine and reached for the receiver. If she lost her job it was no one's fault but her own. She'd made a serious mistake, a grievous error in judgment. If Victoria chose to let her go, Amy certainly couldn't blame her.

"Hello," she said hesitantly, bracing for the worst.

"How are you this morning?"

Mildred.

Amy wanted to be relieved, but it could still be bad news. "Is everything okay?" No way Mildred would miss the desperate quality in her tone.

"Everything's fine here. How are you? I had a moment to catch my breath and I couldn't help wondering if you were doing all right."

Amy dragged the phone back to the sofa with her and reached for the afghan. "I'm okay. Bored, maybe."

"Did you enjoy the chocolates I sent you?" the older woman asked hopefully.

Amy glanced at the nearly empty box of decadent chocolates on her coffee table. "Yeah, they were great." She reached for one now. "Thanks." She popped the delicious candy into her mouth and savored the rich flavor. What did it matter if she gained weight? She was never going to fall in love again. Who needed men? Who needed sex? If she skated through this whole catastrophe with her career intact, she would simply throw herself more fully into it and accomplish the one goal she had left: to become a Colby agent.

At least she had some undercover experience now. Not once had she screwed up and blown her cover. She lifted a shoulder in a listless shrug. That was something, wasn't it?

Of course, if she were really lucky, Victoria would never know about any of it.

"Amy?"

She snapped back to attention. "I'm sorry, what did you say?" She'd definitely zoned out there for a second.

"A position is opening up in research. I wondered if you might be interested. If you are, I could mention it to Victoria. You know, most of our agents do time in research first."

Amy sat up a whole lot straighter. "Mildred! Are you serious?"

"Of course, dear."

Amy could almost hear her smiling on the other

end. "So who got moved up?" Any opening usually meant that someone had been promoted or married and moved away. She refused to think about the two M's. Victoria always worried about losing her people that way. But she gained quite a few in the same manner.

"No one moved up, Victoria just felt it was time to expand the department. She wants someone focusing solely on advanced technology as related to crime solving. You up for the challenge?"

Was she up for the challenge? She'd hadn't spent four years at Chicago State studying the engineering of high-tech gadgetry for nothing. "Absolutely! What do I have to do?"

"Just be here bright and early tomorrow morning ready to dazzle Victoria as to how and why you'd be the best woman for the job."

"I'll be there."

Amy dropped the receiver back into its cradle and jumped up and down, earning herself a rusty creak of disapproval from the sofa's inner springs.

This was just what she needed. A boost. She grabbed the box with its remaining chocolates and hurried to the kitchen to shove it into a trash receptacle. She had to stay in proper physical condition if she was going to reach her career goal. No more feeling sorry for herself. No more worrying about whether she'd meet the right man and have the fantasy.

She'd met the right man, she just couldn't have him. End of story.

REGINA WINTERBORNE touched the handkerchief to her eye, then to her nose, oh so delicately. She couldn't let her mask of devastation slip just yet. The plan she'd devised to garner her father's sympathy had worked like a charm.

He was up in arms over the whole thing. Ready to hang Kevin for fooling her yet again and utterly furious at the young woman from the Colby Agency for not telling someone what had happened so he could have rescued his poor, poor vulnerable daughter.

Regina smiled behind her hankie as her father bellowed those very sentiments to Victoria Colby-Camp herself, the head of the Colby Agency, right that moment. Not that Regina wished poor little Amy Wells any bad will, but someone had to take the fall for this and it sure as heck wasn't going to be her.

However Mrs. Colby-Camp defended her employee or whatever comments she used to smooth over the incident, it was working. Regina could literally see her father calming down, going soft. Regina almost snorted. As long as the woman didn't turn the tide and have her father looking at her with suspicion and indignation in his eyes, Regina didn't care what she was saying to him.

Finally, he hung up and heaved a big breath. "That's taken care of." He settled into his leather, tufted executive chair and peered over his massive desk at her. "Victoria assured me that it was a mistake that won't happen again. However—" her father lifted one eyebrow at her "—she was quick to point out that you used her employee as a distraction."

Regina held her breath, certain she was in big trouble this time.

"But," her father relented, "I know that you were under the influence of that no-good scoundrel Kevin and weren't thinking clearly so we'll let it go for the moment."

She exhaled a little puff of relief.

"But—" he said again more pointedly "—we will square this with the Calhouns. I don't know just yet how I'm going to manage the feat, but I'll make it happen somehow. The question is, can I count on you to do this right this time?"

She leaned forward, her hands clasped in front of her. "Oh, yes, Daddy. I promise I'll be good this time. I'll do exactly what you tell me. John will make a fine husband. I looked at his portfolio and the pictures of his ranch Mr. Beckman sent this morning. It's a lovely place. I could be at home there." She also thought of the dozens of stores and spas located in Dallas that Beckman had told her about. She could be happy there. It wasn't perfect, but it was doable.

She could make it work. Her lips quirked. Besides, if there were any more cowboys in the area who looked as good as John Calhoun she wouldn't run out of distractions. Wasn't there some kind of sports team called the Dallas Cowboys? She would make cowboys her new pastime. And maybe she'd just write herself a book about the joys of living in cowboy country and become independently wealthy.

Her father might force her into this marriage but he darn sure couldn't make her be a wife. And definitely not a mother. The very idea of children made her skin crawl. If Mr. Calhoun thought she'd perform those sorts of duties for him, he'd better wake up, because she was doing no such thing.

Regina Winterborne had no desire to play the role of little wife or mommy. This would be a marriage in name only.

VICTORIA ALLOWED a moment to compose herself after concluding the conversation with Edgar Winterborne. She resisted the urge to shake her head at the man's blind spot where his daughter was concerned. He didn't have a clue how cunning the woman was. Nor did he intend to level any of the blame for this fiasco on her. She was the victim in his opinion. Victoria knew better, but to keep the peace she hadn't pressed the issue.

They had reached an amiable compromise. He let the whole incident go and she would do the same. They would continue to do business in the future as if this unfortunate incident had not occurred. Still, it made Victoria want to kick something.

"Will there be repercussions?" Mildred inquired.

Victoria banished her irritation. She'd forgotten Mildred was waiting to hear the outcome. "None. We're going to call it even and put it behind us. His daughter propelled Amy into the situation and has no right to cry foul.''

Mildred looked immensely relieved. ''Good.''

Victoria's brow furrowed with worry. ''I knew there was something on Amy's mind, but I had no idea she wanted to move into the investigative side of things here.''

Her loyal secretary nodded. ''She's very enthusiastic about it.''

''I'm glad you told me. I believe she'll be an asset. You explained to her that I blame myself partially for this whole incident since I'm the one who stuck that misleading information in with the Calhoun report, didn't you?''

''I did and she's very grateful that you're not going to penalize her for her slip in judgment.''

''Well, there is that. But it was a mistake. One she won't make again I'd wager.''

Mildred nodded her agreement. ''Wisdom is gained through experience, good and bad.''

Determined to know what other surprises might lie down the pike, Victoria decided to go for broke. ''So, how are things with you and Dr. Ballard?''

Mildred smiled knowingly. ''You have nothing to worry about, Victoria. I may take a little time off here and there to enjoy this relationship, but I'll always be back.''

The woman read her like a book. ''As much as I know I shouldn't say this to you, that's a relief. I don't want to lose you, Mildred. I'm not sure this agency could bear the loss. However, I do want you to be happy and I know he makes you happy.''

''You flatter me,'' Mildred countered. ''This agency could survive most anything—except perhaps losing you.'' She eyed Victoria skeptically. ''I know Lucas worries that you spend too much time at the office. And your son needs so much from you!'' she sighed. ''We all worry.''

Victoria had to smile. She deeply appreciated her staff's concern. ''Lucas understands how much this agency means to me.'' It was her turn to sigh. ''Anything my son needs from me is a pleasure not an imposition.''

It wasn't necessary to say more. Mildred knew exactly what she meant.

Love and family were the two most important elements of life. If Mildred's suspicions were accurate, Amy had found and lost that first essential element all in the same weekend.

AFTER CLEARING his schedule for the afternoon John waited in his office for Edgar Winterborne to come on line for the teleconference he'd requested earlier that morning. He'd wanted to discuss the issue immediately but John hadn't been prepared to talk to him just then. He'd needed time and no one was going to deprive him of that. This was far too important a decision.

He'd spent yesterday afternoon and most of last night walking the floors considering all that had hap-

pened…all that he felt. He'd come to only one conclusion where his personal life was concerned: he
wasn't about to jump the gun here. There would be
no whirlwind courtship or marriage. Either Winterborne would go forward with the business venture or
he wouldn't. But John wasn't jumping into a relationship with his daughter.

Not when his heart belonged to someone else.

John steepled his fingers and braced his forehead
there. What little time he'd slept he'd dreamed of her,
every waking moment was filled with thoughts of her.
Even when he attempted to banish all thought of her,
she was still there, just around the corner of his next
thought.

It would take time to get over losing her.

What the hell was he saying? He'd never had her.
She hadn't really belonged to him. It had just felt that
way, that's all. He'd been a fool. Had been blind. All
the signs of deception had been there…he'd ignored
them all.

But memories of the way she'd touched him…the
way she'd looked into his eyes when they made love
had been almost worth it. She'd told him that every
moment had been real to her.

But she'd walked away just the same.

Hadn't given him a chance…hadn't given *them* a
chance.

If it had touched her on the same level as it touched
him, then how could she just walk away without looking back…without calling? Anything?

Then again, he'd let her go, hadn't he?

He'd been too stunned to think clearly, too full of anger about the deception. Now pride kept him from calling her, kept him from risking another blow to his ego.

It wasn't right, he knew. But he—

"Calhoun?"

John jerked from the troubling thoughts and focused on the conference call. "Yes, I'm here."

"Sorry to keep you waiting, but I had a last-minute matter to clear up."

John couldn't help wondering if his daughter had run off with yet another old boyfriend. Nah. He couldn't be that lucky. Then again, he wondered if he'd had employee relations problems at another of his facilities. The PI Nate had hired had learned that Winterborne had a few problems he'd failed to mention during the course of negotiations.

"More problems with disgruntled employees?" John suggested.

The extra second Edgar took before responding told John he'd hit the mark. "Nothing I can't handle in a timely manner."

"There appears to be a pattern of employee-relations problems developing," John pressed. "Is there anything we should know before we continue these negotiations?"

John could almost see Winterborne's face going beet-red and his jowls puffing out.

"As I said, the matter is under control."

He'd just see about that. Nate had orders to keep his PI on the situation. "I'm sure you will. Are we on for tomorrow morning? I'd like to get these plans finalized as quickly as possible and move forward."

Another beat of silence. "We haven't resolved the other matter," Edgar countered. "I'd like this finished. After the fiasco this past weekend, I have no desire to drag out the preparations."

Old Edgar had his heart set on planning a marriage. For some reason he wanted to make sure John was bound to him heart and soul. But he wasn't going to get his way, at least not until John had ample time to determine what he wanted.

His gut tightened, rebelling against the whole idea.

"I hate to disappoint you, Edgar, but that's not going to happen," John told him flatly.

"But...but," Edgar blubbered.

"No buts," John clarified. "I'm not jumping into anything."

"It's that little trollop, isn't it?" Edgar snarled. "She ruined everything with her interference."

John came up out of his chair, sending it banging against the credenza. "Unless you have something constructive to say regarding tomorrow's meeting, this conversation is over," he growled savagely. If he could reach through the telephone line he'd punch the guy's lights out.

"No! Tomorrow's all set. Regina and I look forward to a productive meeting and then a nice lunch. I'll see you in my office around ten."

"I'll be there." John punched the disconnect on his speaker phone and dropped back into his chair. He'd said he would be there. What he hadn't said was whether it was an agreement or a warning. He had a lot more thinking to do before even he knew the answer to that dilemma.

Two quick raps on his closed office door told him his father wanted to see him. No one else knocked on the door, they all buzzed him on the intercom before bothering to show up at his door.

"Come in, Dad."

J.R. sauntered into the room and settled into one of the chairs flanking John's desk. "Your secretary said you were talking to Winterborne."

John nodded. "That's right. We're meeting in his office at ten tomorrow morning. Would you like to go along?"

J.R. grinned. "Any other time I'd say hell no. Don't have much tolerance for the hustle and bustle of that city. But—" he shrugged "—I thought I might just make an exception this time."

Exception, right. He just wanted to know what was going to go down between John and Winterborne. That was the bottom line. The big merger. Making the deal of the century happen.

"Suit yourself." John stood. Sick of the conversation, sick of this place. He needed a little wide-open space to get some real thinking done. "I'm calling it a day."

J.R. got to his feet, then hesitated before taking his

leave. "I thought you might want this." He pulled an envelope from his shirt pocket. "Liam said he found it under the hall table. Must have fallen. *She* left it for you."

John didn't have to ask who *she* was. He stared at the envelope for a long time before he accepted it. Wasn't sure then if he'd read it. He'd already heard her excuses for lying to him. What difference would a written version make?

"See you back at the house." J.R. smiled, but it wasn't his usual high-wattage charmer. This one held a hint of sadness that gave John pause.

"See ya," John muttered. What was eating at him? he wondered as his father disappeared down the hall toward his own office. Not that he needed an office in the building, he pretty much stayed out of the day-to-day operations, showing up for the occasional investors' meeting.

It annoyed John that he was in the middle of this monumental personal crisis and he wasn't even sure whose side his father was on. The company's side probably.

John looked at the letter in his hands and for one second he almost tossed it in the trash, but then he thought better of it. An emotion that was both unfamiliar and overwhelming made him tear it open and stare at the words penned in such gentle, feminine strokes.

The first few paragraphs repeated what she'd already told him of how she'd ended up thrust into his life. He gritted his teeth so hard through that part that it was a miracle the enamel didn't crack. Then the tone of her letter changed.

I don't know how to explain what happened next. I didn't mean for it to happen, definitely didn't expect it, but there it was. Being with you was no longer about the investigation. It was about you and the way you made my heart beat so hard I could hardly catch my breath. It was about the way it felt that first time you kissed me and from there it only got more confusing. I knew what I was doing was wrong, but I just couldn't stop…couldn't leave because to do either of those I would have to let you go.

The letter slipped from his fingers and fluttered down to his desk. Why hadn't she told him that part too? Why had she just walked away?

Because she'd expected the worst…and he hadn't given her the first reason to think otherwise.

John punched in the number for long distance information. "Chicago," he said in response to the request for the city. "Amy Wells." When the operator gave him the number he jotted it down. "Can you give me the address as well?" He quickly scribbled that info next to the telephone number. "Thank you." He hung up.

One decision down.

Chapter Twelve

John scrawled his official signature across the line that would seal the deal of the century. Cal-Borne Alliance was a reality.

Cheers went up throughout Winterborne's office and a cork popped from a champagne bottle. Long-stemmed glasses filled with the celebratory bubbly were passed all around.

Edgar raised his glass and announced, "To a future brimming with prosperity and—"

"Better gas prices!" someone in the back of the room shouted.

"Hear! Hear!" Edgar agreed heartily.

Edgar clicked his glass against his daughter's, then J.R.'s and John's. He took a deep swallow, then added for their ears only, "And to other ventures." He smiled knowingly, glancing from John to his daughter.

"Daddy, if we don't get over to the restaurant, we're going to be late," Regina cooed, then batted her extra-long lashes at John.

He was reasonably sure that lashes that long

couldn't possibly be real. Damn, he hated to waste another hour dealing with her swooning and flirting. One would think the woman could take a hint. He'd all but told her he wasn't interested. Still, she was a persistent little thing.

"You're right, my dear," Edgar crooned. "We'll start in that direction now."

Edgar made several more statements that sent the crowd in his huge office into cheers once more. "Now, if you'll excuse us, Regina and I have to see to the appetites of these two fine gentlemen."

John shook dozens of hands as he was ushered across the room by Regina. She'd snagged his left arm and headed for the door as soon as the words were out of her father's mouth, scarcely giving him time to grab his hat. He could hear J.R. and Edgar accepting congratulations behind them as they followed in the path he and Regina cut through the crowd. The woman was like a bulldozer. She'd set her sights on the door and in no time flat they were through it.

She didn't stop until they stood before the bank of luxurious elevators. Edgar Winterborne had himself one plush set-up here. If this was any indication of his taste, his home likely rivaled a palace. No wonder his daughter was so spoiled. She'd lived in the quintessential lap of luxury.

"I can't wait to come visit you in Texas," she purred, cuddling up to him. "I've heard you cowboys really know how to treat a lady right."

She whispered the last just quickly enough to prevent their fathers from overhearing as they joined them at the elevator.

"We do indeed," John agreed, forcing a smile.

On the elevator J.R. and Edgar made small talk while John tried not to notice how Regina stared at him. The woman hadn't let go of his arm yet and she gave him the once-over at least twice as if she had X-ray vision and could see right through his suit. He hoped like hell she couldn't read his thoughts. Though he didn't much like her, he wouldn't want to hurt her feelings.

Taking the opportunity to disengage himself from her by adjusting his hat into place as they exited the building almost worked, but she grabbed his arm the moment he dropped it back to his side.

"I do love those cowboy hats," she said flirtatiously to both John and his father. If her smile were any wider, her head would split right in two.

John ignored the comment, but his daddy, being from the old school of charm, winked at her and said, "That's why we wear 'em, darlin', to impress the ladies."

John rolled his eyes and resisted to urge to tell her the truth. They wore them to shield against the harsh Texas sun while on the range. He rarely left the house without his boots or his hat, even when traveling. He had left the hat behind the night he'd taken Amy to the country club. The memory slammed into him full force. He'd wanted complete openness with her…

hadn't wanted any mysteries. He pushed away the painful memory.

Several reporters rushed across the parking area to meet them, snapping photographs and asking questions about the merger. Edgar had insisted on keeping the press out of this morning's meeting.

John and his father allowed the Winterbornes to ride that pony. Neither of them had any desire to ham it up. This was business, it wasn't conducted for the notoriety. It was about helping the nation reduce its dependence on foreign oil, and, yes, that was news. But John was big enough to admit that he wasn't about to play the part of hero when his company would greatly benefit from the merger. It seemed a little wrong to him. Let the Winterbornes play the selfless martyrs. This was like everything else in the business world, it was mainly about money. The rest was merely a fringe benefit. To pretend it was anything more would be an untruth.

Damn, he had a hell of a bad attitude this afternoon. He loaded into the limo with the rest. But then, spending time with this bunch, excluding his father, would give anybody a bad attitude.

Whatever else the Winterbornes thought they could still talk him into, they were wrong. No way was he getting hooked up with Miss Spoiled-Rotten here. The very idea that his father and Nate could have believed for one second that he would agree to any such arrangement once he'd met the woman was beyond him. Well, giving them grace, they hadn't met her either.

She was attractive enough. Long dark hair, petite figure. But her eyes gave away the cold-hearted female who lived inside that lovely shell. He'd spent three hours with her and already he knew *this* wasn't going to happen.

Though the Winterbornes had proceeded with the business merger without any further discussion of a "family" merger, John got the distinct impression they still thought it was a possibility.

Lunch went just like the rest of the morning. His father and her father discussed everything from business to the real estate market while John fought off Regina's advances.

Her foot had shimmied its way up his leg about a dozen times, he'd run out of ways to shift to avoid her probing by the time the main course was through.

"Anyone for dessert?" Edgar asked, waylaying the waiter in case anyone wanted to see a menu.

Regina giggled and batted her lashes. John had a feeling her idea of dessert wasn't on the menu. As she grew bolder, her foot slid clear to his crotch.

He scooted his chair back and stood abruptly. "I sure hate to have to run out on you folks, but I have another appointment. Please stay and have dessert on me." He dropped some bills on the table to cover the lunch and tip, then nodded to Regina and her father respectively. "We'll talk again soon."

"Gracious, boy, you're right." J.R. rose and dropped his linen napkin on the table. "The time just clean got away from me.'' He thrust his hand at Edgar. ''Good to be working with you, Edgar.''

Startled that his father had gone along with his abrupt departure, as soon as they were on the sidewalk outside the restaurant John asked, ''Why'd you back me up? You know I don't have an appointment.''

J.R. walked alongside him for a time before answering. ''I almost made the mistake of my life,'' he said finally.

John was so surprised by his statement he stopped to look him in the eye. ''How's that?'' John had his own ideas but he wanted to hear the old man say it.

J.R. looked wearier than John had ever seen him, and worry kicked in. Was there something more going on here than he knew about?

''I was all ready to go along with this whole scheme. Nate was certain it would be the best way to ensure the deal went through.''

Nate. Well, that was what he did. He'd served as Calhoun Oil's top advisor for a lifetime. He knew the oil business inside and out. He didn't miss a trick.

J.R. shrugged. ''It sounded like a good thing. You'd have yourself a wife and we'd close the biggest deal of the century. Considering Edgar Winterborne's reputation, how bad could she be?''

Well, they both had their answer to that one. ''Dad, it wasn't altogether your fault. We all—''

J.R.'s expression hardened. ''It was *my* fault. I almost married you off to that.'' He flung his arm back toward the restaurant. ''I would never have forgiven

myself if I'd saddled you with that kind of heartache."
Shaking his head he started forward again.

John followed. He and his father had not discussed
Amy. In fact, J.R. had remained oddly silent about the
whole affair.

When they'd walked another couple of blocks in no
particular direction, J.R. spoke again. "We have to
make it clear that no personal relationship is going to
come of this merger."

"I've tried to make that as clear as I can," John
countered, "they don't seem to want to take the hint."

"Then we'll just have to tell 'em outright," J.R.
said, his temper rising. "I'll tell them."

John smiled at his father's sudden determination on
the subject. "Why not let Nate tell them?"

J.R. waved off the suggestion. "Hell, I don't want
to give the man a heart attack. I had as much to do
with this as he did, I'll take care of it."

Another period of silence lapsed between them as
they strolled along the sidewalk that grew more
crowded with each block they covered. Shop after
shop and department store after department store dot-
ted the Magnificent Mile. It was just three in the afternoon, still a couple hours before Amy would be off
work, if her schedule was the typical nine-to-five.

John started to tell his father that he intended to see
her when J.R. suddenly spoke.

"The way I see it, we've screwed things up badly
enough. We need to set it to rights ASAP." J.R.
paused again, sending pedestrians scurrying around

the obstacle he made in their path. "You need to find her. Tell her you made a mistake and see if you can work things out."

John stared at his father in disbelief. "You're talking about Amy," he said, just to be sure he wasn't somehow confused here.

J.R. quirked a bushy blond brow. "Now who else would I be talking about? Do you think I didn't notice the way you two looked at each other? The way you've been moping around since she left? Something came to life between the two of you...something special. Don't let it slip away just because she pretended to be somebody else for a couple of days. According to Liam she had her reasons. We all make mistakes. Just look at what I almost got you into."

Liam? Now what did he have to do with any of this? He frowned for a second then realized that Liam had been the one who found the letter.

"I was planning to see her this evening," John admitted. "I can catch a commercial flight back tomorrow."

"Nonsense," J.R. scoffed. "You do what you have to. The plane can stay here with you. I'll take a commercial flight back." He grinned. "It's been too long since I enjoyed the company of a good stewardess anyway."

Who could argue with that?

"All right," John agreed. "I'll see you tomorrow then."

His father did something completely unexpected

then, he grabbed John and hugged him. "Don't let her get away, boy, or you'll regret it for the rest of your life." When he drew back, he looked his son up and down. "I'll call the pilot and Nate and let them know about the change in plans." He scowled. "For God's sakes, find some flowers or chocolates or something. Don't show up at her door empty-handed. Women like that mushy kind of stuff."

John laughed and gave his father a little salute. "Will do."

J.R. was right, John mused, as he watched him flag down a taxi. He couldn't let Amy get away. She was the one. No matter how they'd come to meet or the circumstances that had torn them apart briefly, they belonged together and he intended to see that happen.

Every minute he wasted was a minute he could have spent with her.

Time was too precious to waste.

AMY CLIMBED OFF the bus and quickly covered the two blocks to her apartment building. Taking the bus to work was so easy, driving was pointless, except on Fridays when she went to the bank or on other special occasions. In the empty stairwell, she tugged her mail from the box cursing under her breath. What was it with these mailmen? How did they expect to cram so much into a box and hope the recipient would be able to remove it undamaged?

She smiled in spite of the mail hassle. Today had been her first day in research. Already a temp was filling in for the receptionist who was being trained to be Mildred's new assistant. Life was good.

She ruthlessly squashed the little voice that wanted to remind her of the one thing that wasn't right. She would not think about cowboys or Texas or perfect men or anything else male and sexy.

Career first, career first, she chanted as she climbed the stairs to the third floor. Relationships only got in the way of moving up the career ladder. She truly was a Colby agent-in-training now. She had to focus on that goal. See the goal, reach the goal, was her new mantra.

Banishing the image of the handsome man who tried so hard to invade her every waking thought she took the last step up to the third-floor landing. She would eventually stop thinking about him…stop dreaming about him. A heavy sigh punctuated the realization that she probably wouldn't ever be able to forget him or to completely put him out of her mind. He was there to stay.

She looked toward her apartment door, blinked, then looked again.

He was here.

He smiled, his Stetson in one hand, a huge bouquet of red roses in the other. "Hello, Amy."

Her heart came close to stopping completely. A shiver went through her at hearing him say her name. "H-hello," she stuttered. Why was he here?

The abrupt pound of footfalls on the stairs momentarily jerked her attention in that direction. Lance, her downstairs neighbor, rounded the landing, grinning from ear to ear.

"Amy," he called out to her, "wait up."

Her gaze swung back to John. That heart-stopping smile of his had dimmed.

"Maybe I should have called first," John said, his voice tight.

Lance came up beside her. "Oh, sorry. Hello," he said to John, obviously only just then noticing his presence. "Here's that CD I borrowed from you for my party," he said to Amy. "Thanks, it's the bomb!"

She accepted the returned CD. "I'm glad you liked it." She managed a passable smile though she couldn't come close to mustering her friend's enthusiasm.

Lance waved his arms magnanimously. "*Everybody* loved it!" He sent a nod in John's direction then gave Amy a quick peck on the cheek and waggled his fingers at her. "See ya around." He disappeared as suddenly as he'd appeared. But then, that was Lance. Always on the move.

Amy turned back to her unexpected visitor. His entire posture had changed. He looked ready to bite off somebody's head and spit down their throat. His fingers were crushing the stems of the lovely roses.

"Here," she said, moving quickly to their rescue. "Let me take those."

He relinquished his hold on the flowers but trapped her just as abruptly with that fierce gaze. Her confusion at his sudden change in demeanor cleared with just one look into those intense blue eyes. He was mad as hell. Blatant jealousy glittered like sparkling jewels amid the black thunder of his fury.

"Would you like to come in?" she asked, pretending not to notice his fury.

His mouth worked for a moment before an answer was forthcoming. "Yes," he finally barked.

Oh, he was having some real trouble dealing with his anger. Amy couldn't help a smile. If he only knew. She definitely was not Lance's type. But, she decided with just a pinch of glee, he didn't need to know that right away.

She unlocked her door and pushed it open, praying she hadn't left any undies or other embarrassing items lying around.

After she'd gotten over feeling sorry for herself on Tuesday, she'd given the place a thorough cleaning to keep her mind occupied. So at least there wasn't an inch of dust lying around as there usually was. No empty pizza boxes or laundry in need of folding.

"Make yourself at home." She motioned to her well-worn sofa and quickly darted into the kitchen to find a vase for the roses. She dug around under the sink until she found a glass pitcher that would be big enough. The only vase she had was far too small. There had to be a dozen and a half flowers here, not to mention greenery and baby's breath. While the water filled the large-mouthed pitcher, she watched John wander about her place. She couldn't help wondering how he would see it. It wasn't much. Small, jam-packed with her stuff. But it was comfortable. It was home.

The living room, kitchen and tiny dining area were actually one room with only the bar and overhead cabinets serving as a barrier between the spaces. Down a short hall was her bathroom and a good-sized bedroom. She'd decorated in sort of a funky traditional style. Her old sofa was her favorite piece. She'd found it while she was out junking one day. Had gotten Lance and a couple of his friends to help her get it home. The rest of the stuff she'd picked up at bargain sales and antique shops. She loved an eclectic mix. The very contemporary art scattered here and there provided the funky jab of unexpectedness. She smiled. It was her.

She jumped, startled by the water running over the rim of the pitcher. After pouring out the excess, she dried the exterior and arranged the flowers. It looked spectacular and smelled even better. She placed it on the dining table and turned to the man who'd kindly brought them to her. "Thanks, they're beautiful." What was he doing here? She lost her breath all over again when she dared to consider one particular possibility.

A smile tipped his lips and she was glad to see that those volatile emotions no longer cluttered his handsome face. "Just like you," he said huskily.

Amy's heart skipped a beat and much-needed oxygen came in a hard rush. "Thank you." She had dressed up a little today. She'd wanted to impress her new colleagues in research. The wrap skirt was her favorite, the filmy material with its vivid colors made her feel strong and even a little sexy. The sleeveless blouse fit nicely and had a kind of wrap design as well, but instead of tying, it had a couple of buttons on the side. The V-neck plunged just low enough to show a hint of cleavage but not too much. Her shoes were another funky buy, strappy sandals with just enough of a spiky heel to look feminine.

He'd dropped his hat on her coffee table and he stood there now, his hands shoved into his trouser pockets. "I like your place, it's…" He took another look around and appeared to grapple for the right words. "It's just what I expected."

Not sure how to take that remark, she moved toward him. "Would you like something to drink?"

He shook his head. "I thought maybe we could talk."

Amy was afraid to hope…afraid to even think for a second that he was here because he couldn't live without her. Forcing the silly notion aside, she took a seat on the sofa, he sat down in the chair facing her. His navy suit and pale blue shirt were tailored just for him and looked as freshly pressed as if he'd just put them on. The color highlighted those gorgeous eyes.

He looked away for a moment and dragged in a big breath, then those steady blue eyes leveled fully on her once more. "Amy, I wish I knew all the right words to say to fix…" He shrugged. "…what happened. But I don't. I do, however, know that the time we spent together was special. Very special.''

She sat completely still, afraid to move, to speak, even to breathe for fear of breaking the spell.

''I don't want to pretend that last weekend never happened. I can't just go on with my life acting like we never met.'' He stared at the floor for a moment before meeting her eyes once more. ''Is there some way that we can start this whole thing over again? Get to know each other, see if that special connection is as real as I believe it is?''

She forced herself to remain seated when every fiber of her being wanted to jump for joy. She wanted to dive into his arms and scream *yes*. Fighting to keep a calm exterior she said, ''I'd like that. Very much. How...how would you like to go about starting over?''

Relief flooded his expression, making the devilish grin that slid across his face not quite so devilish but incredibly sexy and sweet. ''I know where I'd like to start, but it wouldn't be the wise thing to do. So why don't you show me who the real Amy Wells is and we'll take it from there.''

Oh, now that she could do.

''It'd be my pleasure,'' she said with a distinctly mysterious air of promise.

She'd make tonight one night that this cowboy would never forget.

Chapter Thirteen

So far Amy had given him the Chicago version of what she'd gotten in Texas. They'd strolled through Grant Park. He had to admit that it was pretty impressive considering it sat on the edge of a large metropolis. The sun still shone high enough in the sky to make the view out over Lake Michigan a spectacular site. Between the elm trees and the unexpected splashes of color offered by the rose gardens one would never suspect that some of the nation's tallest highrises, such as the Wrigley Building and the Sears Tower, were mere blocks away.

Now as they stood admiring the Buckingham Fountain he wondered briefly what was next on the agenda. A gentle breeze from the lake sent a cool mist against their skin. Her long silky hair shifted around her shoulders making him want to touch her. Looking at her with the Chicago skyline in the background he suddenly wished he had a camera and could capture this moment forever on film. She looked so serene and so damn beautiful.

"Next we eat." She looked up at him and smiled. "Chicago style."

The twinkle in her eyes told him that she was truly enjoying being in charge. And, oddly enough, he didn't mind at all. In fact, he kind of liked it.

Rafael's was dimly lit, but Amy knew the place like the back of her hand. The owner claimed that his restaurant was the home of the original Chicago deep-dish style pizza. There were a couple others who made the same claim, but as far as Amy was concerned there was no place on earth like Rafael's. Well, except for the numerous others just like it, all run by the same owner, around town.

She watched John's expression go from curious to hesitant as they entered the biker-themed food haven. She could imagine that he considered the dark, murky atmosphere just a little unsettling, the same way most people did the first time they came here. But the pizza would more than make up for it.

"Let's sit over here." She tugged him toward a booth that looked as if it had seen better days with its cracked Naugahyde seats. The graffiti on the walls and the plastic Italian checkered table clothes all looked authentic.

He slid onto the bench across from her and sat his hat on the seat beside him. "Considering we're not wearing leather and didn't ride in on a Harley, are you sure we're at the right place?"

Amy laughed because she had a feeling he was about half serious. "I'm sure." When the waiter dropped by she ordered an original with the works and a soft drink for herself. She looked to John to supply his own drink request.

"Beer."

"I didn't even ask," she said to him after the waiter had gone, "if you like pizza."

He shrugged. "Everyone likes pizza," he offered without answering her question.

"Everyone likes *this* pizza," she countered.

He settled back in his seat and studied her for a moment. "So this is where you come with your friends like Lance?"

Amy stifled a little smile. "Sometimes." He probably thought this place looked like Lance's style, since he'd been wearing leather pants today and had a number of visible tattoos on his arms.

"You and this Lance date from time to time?" John ventured without looking at her. He pretended to be distracted by the spicy pepper shaker.

"No, we don't date at all. We're just friends." She loved that he was jealous. Then she wondered if he actually realized that he was behaving like a jealous lover. The lover part sent another delicious little shiver through her.

"So you come here just for fun as friends?" he persisted.

She crossed her arms over her chest and tilted her head to consider him a moment before she answered. "No. We come here to eat when we're hungry. The place you and I are going next is where we go for fun.''

His frustration level had just crept up a notch. She saw it in the almost imperceptible pulse of a muscle in his jaw. Sexy as hell, she decided.

He wasn't the only one who could ask the questions. ''You didn't tell me why you're in town.'' She'd been so startled to see him she hadn't thought to ask. It would be nice to think that he'd come just for her, but she had a feeling that wasn't the case.

''We signed the contracts on the merger with Winterborne Industries today.''

She nodded. ''I see.'' Perfect. He'd spent the day with Regina and her father. To her supreme annoyance she felt that old nag of jealousy nipping at her emotions. That's what she got for taking such glee from his discomfort.

''Cal-Borne Alliance officially gets under way next month,'' he went on, seemingly immensely proud of the accomplishment.

''That's good.'' She hadn't meant it to come out so hard and unfeeling, but it had just the same.

''But that has nothing to do with us,'' he said, sensing her displeasure with the subject. ''Tonight is about us.''

Just then the pizza came and cut right though the tension. Amy moaned with pleasure as she bit into a thick, juicy slice with its garden-fresh ingredients and maddeningly delectable crust. She'd have to work out an extra hour at the gym to burn off these delicious calories.

"You're right," John said after swallowing a swig of beer. "This is great."

They ate in contented silence. He was as starved as she was and they'd put away nearly the entire pizza before they were finished.

She was glad now that they'd parked a few blocks away, the walking would help burn off a few of those gazillion calories she'd just consumed. She unlocked the driver's-side door of her small coupe and depressed the unlock button. Though she rarely drove to work, whenever she went out at night she preferred to use her car rather than public transportation.

"What's next?" he asked as he folded his long, lean frame into her compact car.

"Fun," she said mysteriously. She didn't know how he was going to take their next stop, but he wanted to know the real Amy Wells. And she loved the place. She was still a young woman after all. Country clubs were nice, but they were a little stuffy and the music had left a lot to be desired.

There was absolutely nothing about their next destination that could even remotely be called stuffy.

It would be the true test of John's intentions. If he could hang with her on this one, there might just be hope for them. If not, well then, she was pretty sure he'd turn tail and run all the way back to Texas.

JOHN STOOD staring at the massive steel door for a full five seconds before he allowed Amy to drag him inside. Something about the Buddha sculpted into the heavy door had given him pause.

Just what the hell was this place?

He could hear the music.

Two seconds later, his hat in his hand, he stood in a nightclub with a distinctly Moroccan decor, but with odd little idiosyncrasies all around. The first thing to catch his eye were the wall paintings of women in repose. Then there was the long burnished-wood bar lined with stools. Antique light fixtures glittered a thousands shards of light over the couples gyrating on the floor. Around the perimeter of the dance floor were areas that looked almost like drawing-room settings with their Victorian-style easy chairs grouped around metal tables. And if that wasn't enough to mess with a guy's mind, there were long black leather and faux leopard-skin benches that formed groupings. Whoever had decorated this place had been in serious need of medication at the time. Or perhaps he or she had been over-medicated. Whatever the case, he'd definitely have to call it eclectic.

A deejay danced on a platform as what John presumed to be hip-hop screamed from the speakers. The club was definitely laid-back, but there was a wild quality to it that didn't quite fit with his sensibilities. Still, Amy looked excited to be here. He frowned, trying to remember the establishment's name. Oh, yeah. The Funky Buddha.

It was funky all right.

She tugged on his hand and pointed across the room. He followed her gesture and spotted the empty table. God only knew if they could squeeze through this crowd quickly enough to reach it before someone else did.

When they'd taken possession of the chairs and pulled them close so they could speak to each other without yelling, she said, "Don't you just love it?" She smiled and surveyed the couples bumping and grinding on the floor.

"Love it," he enthused, nodding like a wobble-head puppy glued to the dash of a speeding car.

"What's it gonna be?" A barmaid shouted as she paused at their table.

It wasn't until she glanced curiously at his hat lying on the table that he considered just how out of place he must look. This was no place for a cowboy.

Amy ordered a virgin Margarita and he stuck with beer.

He remembered what she'd said about going out with her friends from time to time and he decided that this place looked exactly right for Lance. He would fit in here.

Amy said something but he missed it. He leaned forward and asked, "What?" He could hardly hear himself think, much less hear anyone speak.

"Do you want to dance?" She was already swaying from side to side in her chair to the sexy Latin tune now playing.

Panic slammed into his gut. The two-step was all

that a cowboy like him had ever seen the need to learn. He peered out over the sea of swaying bodies and felt reasonably sure he'd never be able to master moves like that with his clothes on and while in the vertical position.

"I'm not sure that's my speed," he offered apologetically. He hated to turn her down but he hated worse the idea of embarrassing himself as well as her.

"Oh, come on, cowboy." She moved in close, her eyes twinkling with mischief. "I know you've got the right moves. Besides, if this one's not your style give it a minute and they'll be playing something else."

He hadn't meant to be persuaded. He'd considered himself stronger than this...but he'd been wrong.

He was a pushover when it came to her.

The next thing he knew she was pulling him from his chair and in the direction of the undulating throng of dancers. The music was so loud it thumped in his head, in his chest, but the deafening quality faded into the background as Amy began to sway to the beat.

She closed her eyes and moved so sensually it stole his breath. Her hands glided over her body as she swayed and undulated those softly rounded feminine hips. The tempting rise and fall of her breasts jerked his attention upward, made him want to reach out and palm one. Instinctively he moved closer to her, his own body now shifting in time with hers. Slowly another kind of music took over, the sensual tension vibrating between them. The beat slowed and so did their rhythm. Slower, a little more bump, a little harder grind.

The music suddenly stopped. She was planted firmly between his spread legs, her pelvis snug against his, her face mere inches from his own.

"See, cowboy, I knew you had it in you."

He almost kissed her right there. That lush mouth looked dewy sweet where her tongue had slid over her lips, dampening them and at the same time drawing his full attention there. Then someone bumped into him and the spell was broken. She backed out of the intimate embrace and weaved her way through the sea of people. He found her at their table sipping on her drink.

Whatever possessed him that night he would never know for sure, but he danced every dance with her. He didn't let her out of his sight for fear that someone else would take his place. The dance partners on the floor changed practically every time the music did. But he never let her go.

Shortly after midnight Amy figured she'd better call it a night. She did have work tomorrow and John, well, she wasn't sure what he had planned. But it was late and she was tired. A good kind of tired, but tired nonetheless. He'd surprised her tonight. She hadn't expected him to go along with her, to dive in so readily.

"What's next?" he asked as they climbed into her car.

He wore a smile but she recognized the weariness

in his voice. He was an early riser, she imagined he was pretty beat by now.

"Time to call it a night. What hotel are you in and I'll drop you off."

She stopped at a traffic light in time to see the startled look on his face.

"You do have a hotel, don't you?"

If his sheepish expression was any indication the answer was no.

"Actually I hadn't thought that far ahead," he confessed. He gifted her with a smile. "Any place will do."

Amy sighed. She was going to regret this.

"You can stay at my place."

God, she'd said it. There was no taking it back now.

"I wouldn't want to put you out."

She shook her head as she pressed the accelerator to set the vehicle back in motion. "Don't be silly. It's the least I can do. After all, you put me up for the weekend."

He didn't argue further. She couldn't decide if that was good or bad. She mentally compared the length of her sofa with his tall frame. Wouldn't work, she woefully suspected. She'd have to take the sofa and give him the bed.

She parked at the curb around the corner from her building and climbed out of the car. When he'd emerged as well she pressed the lock button and headed toward her building's main entrance. He caught up with her in three long strides.

"I don't mind going to a hotel," he offered again. "It's not a problem."

"Really, John, it's okay." She'd made up her mind, so why did he keep bringing it up? Surely he wasn't as uncertain about all this as she was. A little shiver quivered through her at the idea that things could happen…

No. That wouldn't be smart. They needed to take this slowly.

Inside her apartment she set the deadbolt and tossed her keys onto the table by the door. "Would you like some coffee or anything?" She kicked off her shoes and headed toward the kitchen. Café mocha would be good. She had the instant decaf kind so it wouldn't keep her up and it would be easy.

"Only if you're having something."

Forever the gentleman, she mused. Then she thought about the way he'd moved on that dance floor. She smiled as she reached for the kettle. Who would have thought a straitlaced cowboy like him could move so sensually? She'd known he could do a darn good two-step and there was definitely nothing missing from his love-making moves. But not every man could move like that on a dance floor, especially not in a crowd of strangers to music he didn't even like.

She knew what John Calhoun liked—country music. Beer-drinking, boot-stomping pure country. She'd seen the CDs at his house, noted the tunes he liked at the dance they'd attended at the Runaway Bay Country Club. He definitely wasn't an alternative rocker or even a hip-hopper. But, damn, if he couldn't ooze to a hot Latin beat. Whew! She started to sweat just thinking about it.

"It'll take a couple of minutes," she said as she strode back into the living room, which was, technically, part of the room she'd just left, but the divisions made by furniture and the cabinets made it feel like different rooms. Right now she needed a thick brick wall between her and the cowboy currently dogging her every step. Otherwise she was going to end up in his arms again, only this time they were all alone. No crowd of dancers to keep them from stripping off their clothes and following the instincts of their bodies.

"Do you have a photo album?" he asked as he glanced curiously around the room.

The room just wasn't large enough to allow much distance. And with him only about four feet away, she could feel his pull…that biological man-woman thing. She folded her arms over her chest protectively and tapped her chin thoughtfully. "I don't recall being shown any photo albums at your house," she reminded, any kind of chatter to distract herself. Wasn't this about hospitality? He'd shown her a good time in his home state, now it was her turn. But she wasn't about to give more than necessary. She'd already lost far too much to this cowboy.

He threw up a hand in surrender. "You've got me on that one. I did fall down there." He grinned. "But, I did take you to church with me. Is that one on the agenda?"

She shrugged. ''We could call my mom, but then she'd faint when I told her I needed to go to church. So I guess I can offer you the photo albums in lieu of that.''

John moved toward her, every step deliberate, that blue gaze searing into hers. ''Why, you heathen. Don't tell me you've been remiss in your church activities?''

She sighed. ''Guilty. But I promise to do better.'' And she did. That was something she'd meant to improve upon. Everyone needed some spiritual uplifting occasionally. And it would make her mother happy. She'd been thinking quite a bit about her family lately. Maybe something good had come of her heart-wrenching visit to Texas. His last step brought him into her personal space, entirely too close for keeping her head on straight.

''Amy.'' He took her hands in his. ''Can we be serious for a minute here?''

Her heart stuttered. ''I guess so.'' She so did not want to get her hopes up about why he was really here. She'd spent all evening avoiding the bottom line. Her heart couldn't take another let-down any time soon.

''I've done a lot of thinking—''

The kettle whistled, long and loud, cutting him off. ''I'll be right back.'' She pulled free of his hands and hurried to the stove. Quickly turning off the burner, she emptied the instant café mocha packets into two mugs. When she'd stirred in the hot water, she carefully lifted the cups and carried them to the coffee table. The whole time she chanted a silent prayer that she wasn't setting herself up for another enormous let-down. Once was enough in this lifetime.

He waited until she had taken her seat to settle into the chair across from her. When he would have continued with whatever he'd intended to say she lunged to her feet.

"You wanted to see a photo album."

Giving herself a mental pat on the back she hurried to the bookshelves built into the wall near her television set and picked through the albums until she found the one she wanted. She simply wasn't ready to hear whatever he wanted to talk about. He'd had her as horny as hell for hours tonight. She needed to calm down, brace herself before she allowed any other stimuli.

She sat down on the sofa and spread open the album on the coffee table between them. He scooted the steaming cups aside to make room.

"School years," she told him, flipping slowly through the pages that showed an elementary-school student with long pigtails and well-worn jeans. She'd always been a tomboy. Just had to prove that she could do anything the boys could. Well, most anything anyway.

"You're cute," he teased, affection beaming in his smile. "Those pigtails are something. Did you break all the little boys' hearts?"

"No, but I kicked most of their butts."

"Ouch." John laughed. "What'd your folks have to say about that?"

She puffed out a big breath. "Well, my mom prayed every night that I'd turn into a lady. Finally she just gave up and accepted me for what I am. My dad was just happy I wasn't running around the yard squealing like all the other little girls on the block."

John turned to the next page. "Any brothers or sisters?"

Amy pointed to a photo of her and her three brothers. "Three bratty older brothers."

"No wonder you knew how to kick butt."

For a long while John appeared content to pore through the pages of her past. Amy was definitely happy just watching him. She liked the little crinkles around his eyes when he smiled at something he saw in one of the photographs and the breathy chuckles that made her shiver with desire. He'd tossed his cowboy hat aside and looked totally relaxed for a guy in a suit. A grin widened her lips when she thought again of him on that dance floor in cowboy boots and business suit. He'd definitely risen to the challenge.

She twisted her hands together in her lap to still the fingers itching to tunnel through his thick blond hair. From there her mind immediately conjured the image of his wide shoulders and sculpted chest, bared for her searching hands, the tight rings of muscle that encircled his abdomen, and those long, lean legs. She swallowed at the nebulous lump in her throat. Mercy, the man was gorgeous. The numerous qualities listed on that magazine poll for the perfect male instantly ticked off in her mind.

Oh yes, he was quite the perfect specimen.

But…why was he here?

Was he simply trying to make amends? He could be one of those people who hated to be at odds with anyone. This could be nothing more than a friendly visit to put a good spin on a bad parting.

"Why did you really come here?" It startled Amy when she realized the question had come from her.

His fingers stalled when he would have turned the page and he slowly closed the album. He moistened those made-for-sin lips before meeting her gaze. "You ready to talk now?"

He was right. She was the one who'd been putting off this moment. But it had to come eventually. Better now than when she woke up in his arms tomorrow morning. She was pretty sure that was going to happen. She'd watched the way he looked at her all night. Knew what she felt as well. This whole evening had been spiraling toward that end. Before she opened herself up to that kind of risk again, she had to know.

He leaned forward, braced his forearms on his widespread knees and looked directly into her eyes. "You made me fall in love with you, Amy. No matter what else happened, that's a fact. It doesn't seem to matter that I didn't even know your name or anything else about you. It just happened and I can't pretend it didn't."

She lifted her chin in defiance of her own emotions. Her heart was racing already, her pulse tripping madly. But she had to hear it all. "What about the Winterbornes and the merger? You said the papers were signed today.'' That had to mean they'd come to an agreement and she'd been under the impression that that would include a marriage between him and Regina.

He drew in a deep breath and considered the question for a moment. ''I'd be lying to you if I told you that the Winterbornes didn't still want to pursue the other aspect of the arrangement, but that isn't going to happen.''

Amy held a firm leash on her emotions. Not yet, she told her heart. ''Then they are fully aware of your intentions?''

''They're still in denial, but they'll come around. Regina isn't the kind of woman I'm interested in spending the rest of my life with. She's damn sure not the one I'm in love with.''

''But,'' Amy interjected, still afraid to let go and feel all that was welling inside her, ''you were prepared to marry her. You even proposed to me when you thought I was her.''

''I proposed to you,'' he said pointedly. ''It was you that I fell in love with...you that I want in my life.''

She wanted to believe that. Her hands wrung together more tightly. ''How can you be sure? You don't even know me.''

The smile that lit his face turned those beautiful eyes an even darker, more vivid shade of blue. ''I know you.'' He tapped his chest. ''You've been right here since we first kissed.''

She couldn't say for sure who moved first, but they were suddenly in each other's arms. He held her tight against his heart for a long while before drawing back to peer into her eyes. "I love you, Amy, don't doubt that. I came here for you."

As his lips descended to meet hers she closed her eyes and fell headlong into the kiss. Her arms wound around his neck, urging him closer. His hands skimmed down her back to rest on her bottom. It felt so good to be in his arms once more.

She could stay right here forever.

JOHN WANTED this night to be special. Just pressing his lips to hers nearly undid him. This time he intended to make love to her the right way, slowly, thoroughly and in a bed.

Lifting her into his arms, he murmured, "Where's your bedroom?"

"Last door down the hall." She nipped at his bottom lip. "Hurry, John."

He wanted the fire to build slowly, but that didn't look like a possibility. The moment he settled her on her feet in her room, they ripped each other's clothes off, tossing them this way and that. The sight of her perfectly made breasts, small and firm, took his breath. Those dusky nipples had hardened like tiny pearls. He couldn't help himself, he had to taste her.

His mouth closed around one sweet, taut nipple. She cried out with the pleasure of it. He sucked the firm little tip, nibbled it with his teeth, then soothed it with his tongue. Her body arched against him, her pelvis pressing against his.

As he tortured her other breast he lifted her to him, then slowly lowered her onto the bed. The silky smooth feel of her skin all along his had him ready to explode. He wanted this to last…wanted to make her come over and over again before he went over the edge himself. He ticked off the names of all the players on his favorite baseball team from back when he still had the time for being a sports fan…calculated the wins versus losses from the best season.

It didn't help.

She wrapped those toned legs around him and the battle was over. He had to get inside her now. He positioned himself and plunged forward, sinking swiftly into her tight, slick heat. They cried out together, their kisses muffling the sound. The frenzy kept right on building and building with each thrust of his hips, with each pull and drag of her velvety depths. The sound of their choppy breathing filled the air. Every muscle in his body tensed for the coming eruption. Pleasure coursed through his veins like pure, liquid heat. His heart pounded so hard he wasn't sure he would survive another second, but he kept pumping into her…couldn't stop.

She came first, hard and fast, bowing up off the covers, screaming his name. The sound of it riding the wave of her pleasure touched him as nothing else could. He fisted his fingers in her hair and pulled her closer, kissed those sweet lips and then he bucked into his own completion. The sensation of release jolted his senses, gripped his muscles to the point of pain and then let go, every ounce of tension in his body pouring out of him, filling her with the seed of his heart and soul.

"I love you, Amy," he murmured.

She stared up into his eyes and finally said the words he'd waited so long to hear, "I love you, John."

Chapter Fourteen

Amy moaned, a feeling of satisfaction sinking all the way into her bones. It was morning, she knew, but somehow she couldn't bring herself to open her eyes. It felt glorious just to lie here and think about making love with John. All those wonderful hours throughout the night, then they'd drifted off to sleep wrapped in each other's arms. A wicked memory, him waking her just before dawn and taking her fast and furiously, sent a smile sliding across her lips.

This was the way it should be.

Forever.

She slowly cracked opened her eyes, almost hating to give up that slumberous state of warmth and dreaminess just before allowing that first glimpse of morning light. But she wanted to see him. To revel in that amazing male body, all naked and hard just for her. She wanted to look into those heart-stopping blue eyes and hear him say those four little words again.

I love you, Amy.

She froze.

The other side of the bed was empty. Her hand moved over the rumpled covers. Cold. He'd been gone for a while. Then she saw the note on the pillow.

Pushing up to a sitting position, she shoved the hair back from her eyes and hastily read the note he'd written.

Amy,

I didn't want to wake you…you were sleeping so peacefully. I have some very important matters that can't wait to attend to. I'll call you at the office later. Will you spend the weekend with me? Here or there…it doesn't matter. As long as I'm with you.

Love,
John

She smiled and allowed the tenderness of his words to warm her for a while before she crawled out of bed. Most likely she'd be late this morning, but she'd make up for it. Mildred would understand and she'd square it with Victoria if the need arose.

As Amy showered and prepared for the day a kind of uneasiness began to knot in her stomach. She loved John…there was no doubt. He was the perfect man— the perfect one for her. They had a lot to learn about each other yet and that would take time. Her fingers stilled in their work of braiding her hair. Her married friends had told her she would know when she'd met the *one*. She'd even heard the guys around the office talk about finding that certain someone who changed their whole lives, who made everything different from that point forward.

John was the *one*.

But his home was in Texas. His work was in Texas, discounting this new merger with Edgar Winterborne and even that could be in Texas for all she knew.

Her home was here. Her family. And her career. The very one she'd longed for all these years. She'd finally taken the first step. It was going to happen. It was real, no more dreaming.

How on earth would they ever make that work?

Amy shook off the worry. Right now she wanted to enjoy the feeling of being in love and having that love reciprocated. They could worry about and work out the technicalities later.

After locking the door Amy flew down the stairs and jumped into her car. Too late to catch the bus this morning. Besides, this definitely qualified as a special occasion. Thirty minutes later she was at the office. She planned to stay close to her desk until after John called.

As she exited the elevator the new receptionist, Elaine, offered a bright smile and a cheery good morning. Amy waved a hello and dashed straight to her cubicle. She didn't have her own office yet, but that would come. The research department was a large room with cubicles for the numerous employees. At least it was her own private space. She liked it.

"Morning, Amy," Will called.

He was fairly new, but really smart. He was a part-time law-school student and full-time employee. Amy wasn't sure how he kept up the pace, but somehow he managed.

"Hey, Will."

He sipped his coffee and simultaneously offered her the paper from under his arm. "I'm through with it if you'd like to see it."

"Thanks." She took the paper and tossed it on her desk. With Will around she'd never have to worry about paying for a subscription to the *Tribune*. She'd never seen a guy scan the paper so fast.

After grabbing a cup of coffee and checking in with Mildred, Amy settled at her desk and looked over her list of files to review for the day. Not so bad. Maybe if she got ahead of the game she could slip away early tomorrow. She wasn't sure she was ready to go back to Texas yet. Facing J.R. and Beckman and all those other people would take some courage-building. Maybe in a couple of weeks. But John could spend the weekend here.

As if some intuition had forewarned her somehow her gaze went straight to the headlines on page two like a laser-guided homing device. Winterborne–Calhoun Merger Surprises Entire Industry. Wedding of the Century to Follow.

Amy blinked…read the headline again.

She wanted to rip the paper to shreds! To call the reporter and demand a retraction, but the only thing she could do was to keep reading. Morbid fascination held her in a kind of trance.

…a source inside Calhoun Oil stated that oil tycoon John Calhoun, IV, and Miss Regina Winterborne will be married in a quiet ceremony in Texas, date and time unspecified for security purposes. The happy couple apparently fell for each other during the course of business negotiations. This merger makes the newly formed Cal-Borne Alliance the largest American-owned oil company on the planet.

Amy's eyes moved slightly to the right where she found a shot of J. R. Calhoun and Edgar Winterborne leaving the Winterborne Building, next to that photo was one of John and Regina who were arm-in-arm.

Something shattered deep in Amy's chest…the pain was far worse than that she'd suffered a few days ago when John had discovered her true identity.

How could this be?

He'd come to her yesterday…spent all evening…all night with her. Made love to her. Told her he loved her…invited her to spend the weekend with him.

She stared at the paper. This had to be wrong.

Slowly laying the paper aside, she reached for the telephone. She punched in the number for John's office. He'd said he would call her. It was past nine. He'd either be back in Texas by now or his secretary would know when to expect him. A man of his stature—the oil tycoon—certainly wouldn't just disappear without telling someone his whereabouts.

''John Calhoun, please,'' she said to the crisp, professional-sounding receptionist.

It hadn't occurred to Amy until she'd read that article just how different she and John were. She had no money, just a tiny savings account. She rented her apartment and her ten-year-old car was finally paid for. Her parents were just working-class people and her brothers were all either cops or firemen.

She swallowed tightly. John was rich…really rich. Why would he want her? That uneasiness started to twist in her tummy again. She had nothing to offer…she'd lied to him, pretended to be someone she wasn't.

But what about last night?

Surely that was real.

It had felt real.

Abruptly she remembered John asking her if any part of what they'd shared last weekend was real to her? God, he couldn't have come to her last night seeking revenge!

No. Her heart wouldn't believe that. He wasn't that kind of man. She knew him better than that.

''John Calhoun's office,'' a new voice said.

''I'd like to speak to John, please.'' Amy winced at the truly pathetic sound of her voice. Already she sounded like the dumpee in a recently terminated relationship.

"I'm sorry, Mr. Calhoun is in Chicago this morning."

Amy's mouth felt so dry she could hardly manage the next question. "When..." she cleared her throat "...when will he be back in the office?"

"I'm afraid he won't be back until late this afternoon, would you like to leave a message?"

She had to know exactly where he was. She stiffened her spine and went for broke. "This is Amy Wells from the Colby Agency, I really need to speak with him sometime today."

"Ms. Wells, he'll be in Chicago all day most likely. But if it's urgent I could put a call in to the Winterborne office. They'll know how to find him. He's finalizing plans there."

"That's okay. I'll call back." Amy hung up without saying goodbye. Her throat had closed...tears stung her eyes.

His secretary didn't recognize her name which meant John hadn't mentioned her. He was still in Chicago...was with the Winterbornes right now. Why? The merger was finalized. He'd said so himself... unless, there were other plans to finalize.

Amy squeezed her eyes shut and held on to the edge of her desk until the wave of agony passed. When she could focus again she turned to her work. She wouldn't think about this now. It simply couldn't be true. John wouldn't have lied to her like that. *But you lied to him,* a little voice taunted. Still, she refused to think the worst…yet.

She'd just wait for him to call.

JOHN'S PLANE finally lifted off at noon. It had taken far longer to smooth everything over with Edgar Winterborne than he'd expected. He'd decided he wasn't going to let his father face that battle alone. The man had been hell-bent on marrying off his daughter. Well, if he did, it damn sure wouldn't be to John. He'd seen all he cared to of the young woman yesterday. She was way too wild for him.

A smile tickled the corners of his mouth when his thoughts turned back to Amy. God, he'd hated to leave her this morning. She'd looked so beautiful lying there. It had taken every ounce of courage he possessed to leave her without taking her yet again. He'd lost count of the times they'd made love and still— even now—he wanted her. He'd had to fight the urge to drop by her office and see her before catching his plane.

But if he had he wouldn't have been able to leave. And he had to get his affairs in order before the weekend. He had big plans. He wanted to make this weekend truly special. All he had to do was pull it together. His father could take over things at the office. Nate would oversee the final legal details on the merger. And John would propose to Amy again. This time he wasn't taking anything but yes for an answer.

What felt like a lifetime later his plane touched down in Dallas. He couldn't get a limo fast enough. And then the drive to his office seemed to take an eternity. His blood pressure had to be nearing stroke level. He had less than twenty-four hours to get everything in order. He wanted to be back on the plane by this time tomorrow, headed toward the woman he loved.

The moment he stepped off the elevator on the executive floor of his office building he knew something was very wrong. Greetings were curt, gazes were averted.

What the hell was going on here?

Had somebody died and no one had told him?

His first thought was his father but he knew someone would have found him if his father had taken ill.

His secretary had apparently gone to a late lunch, so John walked straight into his office without bothering to look for his messages.

His father and Nate stood waiting for him, both looking as if the world had ended.

"What's going on?" He tossed his briefcase and hat aside.

"Tell him," J.R. said to Nate.

John frowned. What the hell was this? His father had just looked at Nate as if he were road kill.

"Tell me what?" John looked from his father to Nate.

"I...I can explain everything," Nate stuttered, his flustered expression a first in John's memory. He couldn't recall ever having seen Nate so rattled.

"I'd suggest you get started then," J.R. snarled.

John sent a pointed glare in his father's direction. "Tell me what the hell is going on?"

J.R. grabbed a newspaper from John's desk and shoved it at him. "This is what's going on."

John accepted the paper then straightened it enough to see what the fuss was about. The first thing his gaze landed on was the picture of them coming out of Winterborne's office yesterday morning. That didn't actually surprise him. The merger was big news. Then he read the headlines.

"Son of a…" His words flowed to a stop as his brain absorbed the full implications of the article. "Who the hell printed this bullshit?" Then he saw the name at the top of the page. *Chicago Tribune.*

Amy.

"Tell him what you did," J.R. snapped at Nate. "Tell him or I will."

John didn't give a damn what anyone had done. He had to call Amy. He rushed around behind his desk, ignoring the argument escalating between Nate and his father. He stabbed all the right numbers…he'd already memorized every number that would put him in contact with her.

"Amy Wells, please," he said as soon as the receptionist had finished her spiel.

"I'm afraid she's not in at the moment, sir. May I take a message?"

John hung up without another word. She probably wouldn't take his call. He couldn't blame her. "Who's responsible for this?'' he roared, fury all but devouring him where he stood.

Nate blinked twice. ''I…I am.''

The only thing that kept John from rocketing over his desk and beating the man to a pulp was the fact that Nate was thirty years older than John and he couldn't bring himself to do that.

''I tried to stop it,'' Nate said. He shook his head. ''I thought you were going to ruin everything! I…I was afraid that if you went after the Wells girl Edgar would call the whole deal off.''

''Tell him how you leaked the so-called wedding plans to that reporter. How you told him right where to be and at what time so he could snap that picture!''

John glanced at his red-faced father. They all needed to calm down. Though he'd like to strangle Nate at the moment, risking his father, or even Nate for that matter, having a coronary wasn't worth it. He could fix this.

''I did,'' Nate admitted, shaking his head. ''I thought I was doing the right thing. I thought it would help. I didn't know that you really loved her. I thought it was just an infatuation that would pass.''

John took a long deep breath and tried to think what to do. How to rectify this the quickest. If she wouldn't take his calls…

''I tried to stop it,'' Nate went on. ''As soon as I realized the truth I tried to stop it.''

John held up a hand for him to cool it. ''We'll talk about this later. Right now I have to make this right.''

He looked at his father. "If she saw that paper this morning that means she's spent the entire day believing a lie." He knew just how that felt. He blinked, not certain he could contain the emotion. She'd been so hesitant to tell him she loved him. Clearly, she'd been afraid to believe. "After last night…she has to be…"

He didn't have to say more. "I'll have the pilot fire up the jet," his father said. "What else can I do?"

John scrubbed a hand over his face and thought about that, then he looked from his father to Nate and back. "I'm going to need both of you."

Nate bobbed his head up and down. "Whatever you need, John. I'll help you make this right."

"You're damn straight you will," he said. "Now, let's figure this out."

AMY SHIFTED the papers around on her desk, then reshifted them. She sighed. God, she wanted to go home and just lie down and cry. She closed her eyes and pressed her fingers against her throbbing forehead. Her head ached, her heart ached, and her stomach roiled like crazy. Mildred and Elaine had insisted on dragging her out for a late lunch though she'd wanted to stay by the phone. She'd been ashamed to tell Mildred what was going on. But the woman was no fool, she'd sensed that something wasn't right with Amy. Bless her heart, she'd gone out of her way to keep Amy distracted for more than an hour.

But now she was alone with her thoughts. She still believed in John. She knew how the media could trump up a story. Just because they exited a building together meant nothing. They'd been in a meeting together, that would make sense. And someone who'd heard the rumors that a marriage had, at one time, been in the works could have leaked that info. That didn't make it true.

Amy fished the newspaper from her trash bin and smoothed out the crumpled page. Regina Winterborne was gorgeous. And rich. She had everything to offer. Except a personality, Amy mused. Oh yeah, and morals. She chewed her lower lip. She knew John. He loved her. She was sure of it.

But as the afternoon wore on without a call from him her certainty slipped bit by bit.

At least she still had her job.

She could be happy with that.

It looked more and more as though she didn't really have a choice in the matter.

"VICTORIA, you have a call from a J. R. Calhoun," Elaine said over the intercom.

"Thank you, Elaine." Victoria wondered why Mr. Calhoun would be calling her. To her knowledge they had resolved all issues related to last weekend's little mishap. "Yes, Mr. Calhoun, what can I do for you?"

"Mrs. Colby, I need your help."

The man sounded breathless, desperate almost. She didn't bother to correct him regarding her name. He would have no idea that she'd married. "What is it you need, Mr. Calhoun?"

"My son is on his way there now. I need you to make sure Amy Wells doesn't leave the office."

Now he had her curiosity peaked. "Why would you want me to do that?" Was there something going on that Victoria didn't know about? Obviously.

"Well, ma'am," J.R. said in that unmistakable Texas drawl. "That little filly is going to be my daughter-in-law. I don't think she knows it yet and she might have reason to run scared. So if you'd keep her steady until John gets there, I'd surely appreciate it."

Victoria lifted a skeptical brow. "Well, I'll certainly try, Mr. Calhoun."

"Thank you, Mrs. Colby. He'll be there within the hour, Lord willin' and the creek don't rise."

After Mr. Calhoun had said his goodbye, Victoria hung up and considered that wind turbulence and heavy afternoon traffic once he was on the ground were far more of a concern to John than the creek rising, but she understood what his father had meant.

She pressed the intercom button and asked Mildred to step into her office, and five seconds later she breezed through the door.

"I have that report ready for you." Mildred placed the neatly printed document in Victoria's in-box. "Was there something you needed?"

Victoria eyed her suspiciously. "Actually there is."

Mildred waited, not showing the first hint of uneasiness.

"What's going on with Amy and this John Calhoun?"

Mildred blushed just a little. "Well, I'm not privy to all the details, but I think our Amy is in love with him." Mildred's expression turned pained. "There may be a problem though."

Victoria shook her head. "There's no problem. The gentleman is on his way here now. We're supposed to keep Amy from leaving until he arrives."

Mildred's eyes went wide. "He's coming here? Why?"

Victoria sighed. "He's going to propose, which means we're going to lose her." Oh, hell, there was that true-love thing again. A burst of pink warmed Victoria's cheeks as she thought of Lucas. The Fourth of July celebration hadn't been the only fireworks taking place this past weekend.

"Oh my." Mildred wrung her hands. "That girl is like a daughter to me." She shrugged then. "But if they're in love…"

Victoria waved her off. "I know, I know. Keep her busy until her suitor arrives. We'll just let destiny have its way."

As if she or anyone else could stand in the way of fate.

Victoria smiled. That was just part of the rollercoaster ride of life.

IT WAS past five o'clock. Amy just wanted to go home. Everyone else in research had already gone.

If Mildred thought of one more thing for her to do… She huffed as she ran the last set of copies. This was Elaine's job now. Amy was in research, not in clerical anymore.

She harrumphed. The perfect ending to the perfectly crappy day. At least the menial tasks had kept her mind off—

No, she refused to even think *his* name.

He hadn't called.

For all she knew he could be off on his honeymoon by now.

She furiously blinked at the emotion that tried to brim. Fine. She hoped he enjoyed his life with that…that hellcat. She would make him miserable. Amy couldn't help feeling sorry for him at the thought.

But she quickly tamped down the wasted emotion. Who was going to feel sorry for her? Nobody, by God, because she had her career. She would go on. She didn't need the perfect man. She didn't need the fantasy.

She didn't need anything but work.

''Amy!''

She rolled her eyes. Mildred. If she had more copies to run, Amy was just going to walk out without even saying good-night.

She set the stacks of copies in the bin for Elaine to pick up tomorrow and dusted her hands off. At least she was through with that enormous pile. Now, to see what the heck Mildred wanted this time.

She marched into the lobby ready to hunt down the sweet old lady and tell her to give it a rest.

Amy drew up short just inside the door.

Roses.

Red roses.

Everywhere.

Dozens upon dozens of huge bouquets, all lavished with greenery and baby's breath. All embellished with enormous red bows.

"I think I have some explaining to do."

She swung around to face the man who'd spoken. John had just walked out of Victoria's office. He wore his usual designer suit, but the Stetson was nowhere to be seen. And there was that smile. Breathtakingly gorgeous.

"John." The word came out a whisper…a thought spoken.

He was here. And no sign of that witch Regina. And all the flowers. She looked around the room. "What is all this?"

He moved toward her, taking her hands when he paused in front of her. "It's to make up for Nate's mistake. He was the one who orchestrated those headlines. He didn't mean to hurt you…he just got caught up in the fever of the merger. I don't want you to be sore at him…I know it's a lot to ask, but, deep down, he's a good man."

Amy was having trouble focusing, her mind was awhirl with confusion and…happiness. "So you weren't with Regina this morning when I tried to call you?"

A frown furrowed across his handsome brow. "You tried to call?"

She nodded. "Oh, but I didn't leave a message."

"I was with Edgar Winterborne most of the morning. I wanted to be sure that he understood that business was all his family and my family have in common. I didn't want any questions where you and I stand."

"Where do we stand?" she managed to ask, in spite of her heart pounding so hard she could scarcely hear herself think.

He dropped down onto one knee. "I'll ask you again." He smiled and reached into his jacket pocket and withdrew the most beautiful ring she'd ever laid eyes on. "Amy, would you be my wife?"

For two beats she couldn't speak, then an awful reality crashed in on her new bliss. "But where will we live? I don't want to give up my job. I...I..."

He squeezed her hand in his. "Not to worry. We'll get a house here as well. I'll manage. I have reliable folks who can run things in Texas when I'm not around."

"But..." She had to be sure he understood what her career entailed. "Later I may be away for days at a time on assignments."

"I'll take advantage of those times to work around the ranch. Otherwise, I'll set up an office here. With this new merger, it'll be necessary anyway."

She started to tremble. Tears pushed past her lashes. She was very close to being overwhelmed.

"So, is it yes or no?" he asked tentatively.

She might be tied in knots emotionally but Amy knew exactly what she wanted. "The answer is yes!" She wanted John Calhoun. She wanted the fantasy. She wanted it all.

Cheers and thunderous clapping rent the air as Victoria, Mildred and a dozen other Colby Agency personnel spilled into the room.

John stood and pulled her into his arms. "Good answer," he whispered, and then he kissed her.

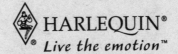

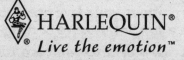

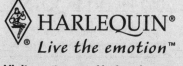

HARLEQUIN®

AMERICAN *Romance®*

proudly presents a captivating new
miniseries by bestselling author

Cathy Gillen Thacker

THE BRIDES OF HOLLY SPRINGS

Weddings are serious business in the picturesque town of
Holly Springs! The sumptuous Wedding Inn—the only place
to go for the splashiest nuptials in this neck of the woods—
is owned and operated by matriarch Helen Hart. This no-
nonsense Steel Magnolia has also single-handedly raised
five studly sons and one feisty daughter, so now all that's
left is whipping up weddings for her beloved offspring....

Don't miss the first four installments:

THE VIRGIN'S SECRET MARRIAGE
December 2003

THE SECRET WEDDING WISH
April 2004

THE SECRET SEDUCTION
June 2004

PLAIN JANE'S SECRET LIFE
August 2004

Available at your favorite retail outlet.

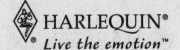

HARLEQUIN®
Live the emotion™

Visit us at www.eHarlequin.com